I0552305

SHIP

by

Prudence MacLeod

Copyright 12/15/2018

Cover art by Thomas Budach

Chapter #1

Shifted

The two armored combatants faced off again as the taller surged back to his feet. They circled each other, watching for an opening. Suddenly he feinted with his left then attacked from the right, but his smaller opponent had read the move. She ducked low and felled him with a leg sweep.

He landed hard on his back and groaned as he unstrapped his helmet and slowly stood up. She'd backed off and was signaling him to come at her again. The man tossed aside his helmet and began to unfasten the armor as he turned his back and walked away. "Hey, come on, we're not done."

"I'm done," he grumbled as he pulled off the armor then left without even glancing back at her.

Sheila Singh, Chief of Security, sighed, watching with mixed emotions while her lover left without another word. "Yes, I guess you are at that." She was reaching to remove her helmet when the ship suddenly lurched and spun, sending her flying.

* * * * *

The mighty starship, Reacher, began to slow her speed as she neared the binary star system that was her destination. Her passengers and crew, the last surviving humans in existence, gathered round the available view screens, anxious for the first look at the new system. As the ship dropped to sub-light speed she was suddenly rocked violently.

The ship bucked and spun about a few times, then was still. Her commander, Admiral Suvi-jean Sorenson began shouting orders as she picked herself up off the floor. "Damage report, all departments."

"Engineering here, Admiral," came the voice of Chief Engineer Moira Duncan. "We've got a hell of a mess, several injuries, but no hull breaches reported, and no atmo leaks."

"Medical here, Admiral, we've got a lot of injury reports coming in, but no deaths as yet. I'll have you some numbers as soon as we get it under control." With that Carla Marks, Chief of Medical, clicked off and went back to work.

Security Chief Sheila Singh was next. "Security here, Admiral. We'll work with medical to get things sorted out. More later."

Jeannie sighed and turned to her second officer who was rubbing his head. "Emmet, what the hell just happened? Where are we?"

"I have no idea at all, Admiral. I'll know more as soon as we get ..."

"Sensors back online, Commander," came a voice from beneath a control panel.

"Well done, crewman. Where are we, Anita?" grinned Commander Jones, as he turned to sensors.

The woman at the sensor panel shook her head as she gazed at her screen. "I have no idea at all, Commander. We're supposed to be in a busy area of space, close to the binary stars, but we're well out in the deep dark. I can see a few faint stars and only one within easy reach. It's a single star, eight planets, perhaps two in the goldilocks zone."

Admiral Sorenson was right at her shoulder. "You're right, we're a long way from where we expected to be. Take your time, see if you can figure out where we are in relation to where we should be."

"Yes ma'am."

Jeannie smiled and turned back to Commander Emmet Jones, the man who was the heart and mind of bridge operations. "Emmet, are we at a full stop?"

"We are, Admiral."

"All right, hold us here for now, get the bridge back to top form; then see what you can learn of what happened, where we are, and what you think we should try next."

"Aye, Admiral."

Suvi-jean sighed and walked off the bridge, heading for her briefing room. She stopped in the corridor and checked in with each and every

SUVI, making sure they, and Sessas, were all right. She then turned her attention to the Earalith. Jeannie finally arrived at the briefing room to find her lady companion, Captain Amanda Drake waiting for her.

"Jeannie, what happened? Are we okay?"

"I have no idea at all what happened, Mandy, but the Reacher seems to have survived. It'll take a bit of time for everybody to get things under control, then I'll call a full senior staff meeting, plus captains and passenger reps. The senior staff can bring us up to speed, then we'll see where we are from there."

"Where we are is halfway across the galaxy from where we started this morning, Admiral," said Commander Jones, as he limped through the door. "Thought I'd find you in here. Computer, display visual of known galaxy." A hologram of the slowly spinning galaxy appeared over the long table.

"Here's where we were, as we came out of hyper drive and went sub-light. Here's where we are now, just off the tip of this arm of the galaxy."

"Good gods, Emmet, are you saying we jumped from one arm of the galaxy to another?"

"Yes."

Jeannie gave a long slow whistle as she sat back in her chair and reached for Amanda's hand.

Amanda was gazing at the chart. "Commander Jones, can you tell me something. We poor humans believed ourselves to be alone in the universe until Jeannie showed us the Earalith colony. Since then, we've encountered a lot of evidence of other forms of life. Why is that; do you know?"

He smiled as he reached to point at the chart. "Well, Captain Drake, it seems that Earth is over here somewhere, a bit isolated. Even in the years we explored, we didn't get too far from home, galactically speaking.

"Now, the Earalithian empire was huge, and roughly over here where we finally brushed up against their territory at Elysium. Since then, we moved in this direction, away from Earth and deeper into Earalith territory."

"And now we're way over here?"

"Apparently so. We must have passed through some kind of rift in space/time."

"Can we go back, Emmet?" asked Jeannie.

"I can't imagine how, Admiral. All our sensors tell us everything is normal out there in all directions. Whatever tossed us over here, left no sign of its existence."

"Well, if we can't go back, then we must then go forward. As soon as the ship is ready for travel, we'll proceed to that nearby star system Anita found."

He smiled and nodded. "I'll get everything organized on the bridge. We'll be ready whenever you are, Admiral." With that he saluted and limped out of the room.

Amanda sighed and sat back, still tightly gripping Jeannie's hand. "It's driving you nuts too, huh?"

"What?"

"The waiting, it's driving you nuts too. The toughest part of being the captain is telling the others what has to be done then waiting for them to do it."

Jeannie chuckled at that. "Yes, it makes me crazy. This being Admiral Sorenson has a few drawbacks, I'm itching to go do something, but I don't want to undermine the confidence of the people I've put in charge. What do I do now?"

"You've waited long enough, you can do walkabout now," said a voice behind her.

She turned to see her grandfather, Frank Baris, the former captain of the Reacher, smiling at her. "Grandfather?"

"I assume that as soon as the event happened, you were on the bridge issuing orders, contacting the various departments for reports, yes?"

"Yes."

"So, it's been a while now since we were tossed about, now you visit each department, get a report, express your confidence in your staff, look for other issues, then tell them to carry on and to keep you informed."

"Is that necessary?"

"Not actually, but it'll keep you from going crazy, and it'll let the crew and passengers relax a bit to see you being personally involved. Jeannie, they need to see you, a fully relaxed and confident you, moving about the ship.

"Amanda, you should be with your crew at your new ship as well."

"Is that where you're going, Grandfather? To your new ship?" asked Jeannie.

"Indeed so. I just thought I'd swing by here in case you were hiding out."

"Hiding out?"

Frank Baris smiled and sat down beside his granddaughter. "Jeannie, you've had your confidence shaken a few times lately, first when I got into trouble, and again when Jake got lost on the planet you named Stormy. Yes, Amanda and Linsey are amazing with their ships and crew, but this is the Reacher, your ship, your crew. You need to get out there and take command."

Jeannie reached over to lightly kiss his cheek. "You're right, Grandfather. Thanks for the pep talk."

"Just doing my job as your mentor." He smiled and patted her shoulder as he rose and walked out of the room.

Jeannie rose to her feet with a liquid grace. "He's right, Mandy, we've got work to do." Amanda smiled and gave her hand another squeeze, then fled the briefing room.

Chapter #2

Damage

Jeannie walked onto the bridge to find her first officer, Brandon Hoffman, in conference with the second officer, Emmet Jones. "Gentlemen, tell me good things. Brandon, what's our current status?"

"I have good news and bad, Admiral."

"Give me the good."

"The outer hull suffered no damage at all, none. For whatever reason, it was unharmed by the anomaly."

"Good to know, now hit me with the bad."

"We were spun around so fast there was a lot of internal damage, mostly to the passengers and crew, as well as whatever wasn't fastened down. Engineering's shipbuilding bay took a beating, stores as well.

"Medical has sealed off Sanitation while the crews are patching up the damage there. That's being cleaned up, and the mess as well now. Eamon's overseeing the work and won't break that seal until he's certain no contamination will ensue.

"The rest is bits and pieces. The main areas of concern are Medical and Engineering."

"Stay with it, Brandon. Emmet, how are we here?"

"Ship is holding steady as ordered, Admiral. Bridge is fully functional and ready. We've been making some long-range scans to confirm our location, but it appears as though we are exactly where I told you before. We're a long way from home."

"No, Emmet, Reacher is our home, the only one we've got. It makes no difference where she is, she's home. However, I get what you mean. We have now entered the realm of uncharted territory. Where we were, we had the remains of the Earalith Empire, their knowledge of that area of space plus their tools, tech, and metals. That's a valuable resource we've lost.

"Ah well, can't be helped. I'll go check in with Engineering now. Let me know if anything new arises." With that, she left the bridge.

Halfway to Engineering she was met by Miriam Holbrooke, President of the Passengers Association. "Greetings, Miriam. You look like you've had a rough morning."

Miriam gave her a weak smile. "Very funny, Admiral. Dare I ask what happened?"

"We hit some sort of rift in space/time, got thrown around a bit, but we're still in one piece. The main hull suffered no damage, but inside is in a mess. I'll call a full top-level meeting as soon as we get things settled down. I'll want you to be there."

"Thank you, Admiral. I also have another request."

"Oh?"

"Yes, a lot of our people want to help with the cleanup. It's easy to see what needs to be done, want some help?"

Jeannie smiled with relief. This was so much better than the way things once were, this could help bridge the gap between the passengers and crew. "Love some, hang on." She reached for her comm button. "Sorenson to First Officer."

"Here, Admiral."

"Brandon, Miriam's here with an offer of help from the passengers. Could you use a few more cleanup crews?"

"Indeed I could. Tell Miriam I'll meet with her and the volunteers, Mess #3 in ten minutes. Oh, tell her thanks."

"I'll do that. Sorenson out."

Miriam Holbrooke smiled with delight. "I'll go gather a few volunteers then meet Brandon. Thank you, Admiral."

"Thank you, Miriam, this could help ease a lot of tension between passengers and crew."

"That was my thought as well," she said, as she walked briskly away.

Jeannie smiled to herself as she proceeded to Engineering. The place was in complete chaos, or at first glance it looked like it. She lost her smile as she surveyed some of the carnage. There was blood spatter everywhere, broken tech, parts, tools, and more scattered around.

Spotting the admiral, the Chief Engineer Moira Duncan, came hurrying over to her.

"Moira, give it to me in small pieces."

"Aye, Jeannie. Unfortunately, this is a place with a lot of moving parts, most of them harder than a human. As things flew around, a lot of people got hurt, some badly."

"Understood, Moira. Now give me the state of the Reacher's vital systems."

"All damage to the Reacher's vital systems has been patched up. As soon as I get a few of my people back to work we'll get those repairs done properly. As it is, the ship can function, but I wouldn't jump to super light speed yet."

"So, we're good for the moment?"

"We are. The air and water processors took a hit. We've got the air back up to fully functional, but we lost a lot of water before we got that leak plugged."

"Is this a problem? Do we need to ration?"

"No, I don't think so. We've got a few more repairs to go on the water purifiers then a day or so to bring everything up to par, but we should be good."

"Okay, so what aren't you telling me?"

Moira Duncan sighed and allowed her shoulders to slump. "Your fleet just got smaller."

"Explain."

"Jeannie, a lot of things, important things, got broken. We're using up our reserves and a lot of our materials, fabricating replacements. I want your permission to scrap one of the new ships. I need that metal."

"Do it, Moira. What will that leave us with for small ships?"

"The two Friendships are good, Explorer Two, or EX2 as we call her, will be ready as soon as her crew gets her cleaned up. Recovery One and Recovery Two are good to go, EX3 is still a possibility, but EX4 will need to be scrapped."

"So we'll have one, possibly two, explorers, two salvage ships, and two Friendships. Not so bad as all that. Do what you have to do, Moira. I'll go check in with the captains." She stepped carefully as she approached Friendship One. The admiral knew well that everyone was trying to keep out of her way, but she didn't want to slow them down in their tasks.

"Greetings, Admiral," sang the cheerful voice of Captain Linsey da Silva, the Chief of Alien Relations and captain of Friendship One.

"You seem happy, Linsey."

"I am, Admiral. Friendship came through the shake-up unscathed. It seems he sensed the sudden change in his environment and braced for impact. I've already checked in with the crew and everybody is fit for duty. We've got a few bangs and bruises, but we're good to go. We'll have him all tidied up in a jiffy."

"Good news indeed, Linsey. When you say he braced for impact, what do you mean?"

Linsey smiled as she explained, her pride in her ship evident. "Ship raised his shields and increased internal gravity to max. Nothing hit the hull and inside not much was tossed very far. Made for an easy clean up."

"I'm impressed, Linsey, carry on."

Jeannie continued on to Recovery One. "Olga, good to see you in one piece."

Olga Volkov, captain of Recovery One, smiled in return. "Hi Jeannie, yes, I'm in one piece, and apparently, so is my ship. I'll be short two crew for a few days, but all's well here. We'll be shipshape in no time at all. Any idea what happened?"

Jeannie told her. Olga gave a long slow whistle then sighed. "All right then, it appears we have new places to go, new things to see and do. You know, Jeannie, I was about to retire before you came along. I was bored. We went years sailing through space and not a single thing happened to break the monotony. You came riding aboard the ship on that monster and it's been one thing after another ever since."

Jeannie grinned. "I try to please."

Olga chuckled at that. "Jeannie, you've breathed new life into a lot of us, and that's not a bad thing. Now, Frank's over there trying to tidy up Recovery Two. You'd better check, I think I saw him loading that old speeder of his onto the ship."

"He's determined to break his neck with that thing," sighed Jeannie. "Carry on, Olga, I'll go see what mischief your compatriot is up to." Captain Volkov chuckled as the admiral walked away.

Jeannie peered up the ramp to Recovery Two. "Hello, Captain Baris, permission to come aboard?"

"Granted. Welcome, Admiral Sorenson." He grinned as his granddaughter approached up the ramp. "Tell me, did Olga rat me out about the speeder?"

Jeannie chuckled. "She did. Grandfather, you'll kill yourself with that thing."

"Well, I won't try to ride it on the ship. I just thought, you know, if we happened to be groundside, you know, with a bit of open space ..."

"You're doing this just to worry me, aren't you? Chance Morita, is that a uniform I see you wearing?"

"It is, Admiral Sorenson. Captain Baris offered me a job where I get to play at salvage and more. How could I resist?"

"Indeed, well then, as your admiral, I have a special task for you."

"Oh?"

"Yes, keep your captain from breaking his neck with that damned old speeder of his."

Chance Morita grinned with mischief. "I'll keep a close eye on him, Admiral."

"You're as bad as he is," sighed Jeannie. "How's your ship, gentlemen?"

"The Earalith built them tough, Jeannie," smiled her grandfather. "We'll have him tidied up and ready for service in no time at all."

"Good to know. Carry on, gentlemen, keep me informed." With that she walked away, headed for EX2.

She found Amanda with the second-in-command of Security, Sub-Commander Jake White, her self-appointed big brother. "Hi guys. Jake, how are the wives?"

"Busy," he replied, then sighed as he saw the grin on her lips. "It's not funny, Jeannie."

"Getting teased a lot about the three wives?"

"You could tell?"

Jeannie laughed and gave him a gentle punch on the arm. "Folks will get used to it."

"Yeah, I know, and it's only two wives. In truth I don't see a lot of Sessas, she sticks pretty close to Friendship One or with Hal and Lilly."

"Hal and Lilly?"

"It was Hal who figured out she's an adult, not a kid. He trusted her with weapons and backed her up, that counted big for her. Carla is up to her ears in Medical right now, and Twenty's been spending a lot of time with Harlan down in his workshop."

Jeannie had a twinkle in her eye. "Jealous?"

"Stop it, Jeannie. Cripes. No, I'm not jealous, but I'm a little worried. She says she's working on something important but won't say anything more just yet. That woman is up to something."

"She usually is," chuckled Jeannie. "Mandy, how's your new ship?"

"We were ready for test flights before the event happened. We've got a few fixes to make, but nothing serious. Moira tried to build her as tough as the Friendships. That looks like a huge success. EX2 can take a beating all right."

"Good to know. Get her ready, Mandy. I want those test flights done as soon as possible."

"Will do. Jeannie, what's going on?"

"We've been hit, beat up, and now we're licking our wounds. I really want to see something, anything, happening that looks forward, something positive. Those test flights will divert a lot of worry and uncertainty from the state of the Reacher."

"You want us to check out that nearby system?"

"Not just yet, but soon."

"You're the distraction, Mandy," said Jake. "Right now the entire ship is on the edge of panic because of what happened. If Jeannie can create a fuss over the new explorer ..."

"It'll take everybody's mind off what happened, give them new hope that things will go on and get better. Got it." Amanda grinned as she reached for her comm. "Attention, all EX2 crew, assemble and prepare for test flight pre-flight checks."

Jeannie grinned at her. "You accidentally let that go out over a general call. Everybody on the ship could have heard it."

Amanda matched her grin. "Ah-huh."

"You're tricky; well done, sweet Mandy. All right, you've got this. Carry on, I'm headed for Medical."

The Admiral walked into the Medical bay to apparent mass confusion. There were a lot of people on stretchers with medics weaving through the confusion. Carla Marks, Chief of Medical, was in the middle, directing traffic as stretchers were moved around and people transferred to beds, or bandaged up and released.

Jeannie moved over by the door to Carla's office, so as not to be in the way. Carla spotted her there and raised her hand, one finger extended. Jeannie nodded and stepped into the office. A few minutes later Carla joined her, sighing deeply as she sank into her office chair.

Jeannie gave her a gentle smile. "Busy day?"

"Somewhat. What the hell happened?"

"We got caught in a space/time rift and tossed halfway across the galaxy."

"Seriously?"

"Seriously."

"Damn, Twenty was right again."

"Excuse me?"

"Last night she said she had a bad feeling. Later she sat up in bed and shouted a warning. 'Grab onto something.' By the time that registered, we were spinning out of control. I'd have been thrown across the room, but she held me in place with one arm and pinned Jake with a leg. Sure is handy having a super SUVI for a wife.

"Now, you want a report. I don't have the final numbers yet, but on the bright side, no fatalities so far. Lots of injuries, many serious, but no fatalities.

"I found Dr. Reilly and his new girlfriend staggering out of quarters and put them to work supervising the cleanup at Sanitation. Everybody there is in enviro suits and Dr. Reilly has them locked down. He'll make certain it's secure before he breaks the seal.

"Outside that, there's not much more I can tell you at the moment."

"I can see you've got things well in hand, Carla. I told you I chose the right woman for the job." Carla smiled and chuckled at that. "Now tell me how you're doing."

"I'm fine, Jeannie, a little tired, but no problems."

"That's not what I meant, girl, and you know it."

"Yeah, well, okay, I'll talk. I know it was my idea to bring Twenty into the marriage with me and Jake, but it was the only real solution, and we all know that."

"Not working out so well?"

"No, Jeannie, on the contrary, it's working out better than I'd hoped. Yes, it was awkward at first, for all of us, but the funny part of it is, it's Twenty who's the glue that holds it together. That intuition of hers is amazing. She knows what you're feeling before you do. Anyway, she's easy to love, and I'm getting there a lot faster than I'd hoped. The hardest part is Jake."

"Jake?"

"The poor guy is terrified he'll show too much affection for one of us and the other will get jealous. Don't worry, Twenty and I'll bring him around, loosen him up a bit."

Jeannie chuckled at that. "Carla, I truly believe you are all right with this arrangement."

"Yeah, I am, Jeannie. I mean, we're all raised to believe it should be only two people to a marriage, and for most people that's the way it works, and I thought I was one of them."

"But?"

"But I was forced into something else, and I learned something quite wonderful."

"Oh?"

"Yes. The heart has the capacity to love many people, all at once. Love isn't a piece of pie that you lose some by sharing, it's a magic pie that always has more for you the more you share. I mean, I can see how much Jake loves Twenty, and how deeply she loves him, but I can also see how much they both love me.

"They couldn't fake that with me, I'd know the difference. By giving myself permission to love them both, it was easy. As soon as I let go of the idea that it wasn't possible and just went with it, bang. I can't imagine ever being without either of them."

"What about Sessas?" grinned Jeannie.

"She spends a lot of time with Hal and Lilly. She sure is a lovable character though. She has a way of looking at you that just makes you want to smile. Jeannie, I'm good here, I am. This three-way marriage is working, we're growing closer every day."

"Then I'm at peace, dear friend. I'll head over to Stores now and let you work."

"Thanks for checking up on me."

Jeannie patted her shoulder then walked out, heading for Stores to survey the damage there.

Chapter #3

Taking Stock

"All senior staff to the bridge briefing room. All captains to the briefing room. Passenger representatives to the briefing room." There was a hurried exit from work areas as the people responded to that call. The two passenger reps were especially eager, for there were far too many rumors afloat. They needed answers.

"Looks like everybody's here, Admiral."

Jeannie stopped pacing and resumed her seat at the head of the long table. "Thank you, Brandon. Very well, let's begin. First Officer, tell us what happened."

Brandon Hoffman sighed as he leaned forward, resting his elbows on the table. "The truth is, Admiral, we're not exactly sure what the hell happened. Best guess, we hit some sort of rift in space/time and got tossed halfway across the galaxy. Emmet, call up the chart and show them where we are."

"Aye, sir." Emmet Jones rose to his feet as he called for the star chart. "Computer, display three-dimensional chart of known galaxy." The slowly spinning mass of pinpoint lights appeared over the table. "We were here, aiming for this binary star system when we came out of hyper drive and went sub-light.

"That's when we hit the rift. It tossed us over here to our present position just off the tip of this galactic arm."

Miriam Holbrooke rose to her feet. "You're not serious, that can't be possible."

Emmet smiled gently as he responded. "Sadly, ma'am, it's not only possible, but it's true. We've spent days trying to reconfigure our star charts from this point, and there's no doubt as to our position."

"Dear god in heaven," sighed Miriam, as she sank back into her chair. "Are we all right? Can we get back?"

"That's what this meeting is about," said Jeannie. "Second Officer, is there any sign of the rift that brought us here?"

"No, Admiral, no sign of anything at all out there."

"Thank you, Emmet. All right, now that we know where we are, Brandon, tell us how we are."

"We're a bit beat up, Admiral, but we're in good shape, all things considered. I'll leave the details for the department heads, but in general we're all right. The ship took no damage to the hull, all vital systems are functioning, there were injuries, but no fatalities, so I'd say we got lucky. We could have been tossed well out between galaxies with a lot more damage."

"Good to know. All right let's get to the bad news. Engineering, report."

"Aye, Admiral. The Reacher's hull is intact, no damage at all. Air and water processors have suffered a lot of damage but have been repaired and are operating at full capacity. We lost a lot of water, but the condensers and processors are working at max and water is almost back up to full capacity. The air scrubbers took a pounding, hence the headaches everybody got for a couple of days, but those repairs are complete, and air is back to full.

"The ship building area took serious damage and we're slowly getting that cleaned up. EX2 has exceeded all expectations on test flights, Friendship One and Friendship Two are good to go, as are Recovery One and Recovery Two. EX3 is a possibility still, but with all the injuries we're a bit short-handed. That ship will be on hold for a while."

"And EX4?"

"Sorry, Admiral, I did have to scrap that one. We needed the metal for fabricating parts for Reacher."

"Understood. Our current status?"

"Reacher is back to full readiness, Admiral, but I'd like to have a few more days to double and triple check the engines."

"Take whatever time you need, Moira. Let me know when we're ready to travel."

"Captains, what is the status of your ships?"

"Friendship One and Friendship Two are fit and ready, Admiral," said Linsey.

"Recovery One and Recovery Two ready for duty, Admiral," replied Olga Volkov.

"Medical?"

Carla Marks sat up straighter in her chair as all eyes turned to her. "Yes, Admiral. Three hundred eighty-seven injuries worthy of mention, many somewhat superficial, others not so much. Three hundred sixty-nine will make a full recovery, eighteen will not. Sixteen of those will be able to return to duty even with some impairments, two will not."

"Carla?"

"One is completely paralyzed and the other has irreparable brain damage."

Jeanie sighed and sat back in her chair. "Distressing news that, but in truth, it could have been a lot worse. Thank you, Carla. Eamon, anything from medical research?"

"A lot of my work got trashed, samples destroyed, etc., but nothing I can't duplicate. I supervised the cleanup and repairs in Sanitation. We're all good there. The only bad thing is the viable embryos we had. We lost a few of them. I'd say we have barely eighty left of the original hundred."

"That's a loss to our gene pool. Call for volunteers, Eamon. Get as many of those into our gene pool as you can. Security, report."

"All's well on the security front, Admiral," smiled Sheila Singh, Chief of Security. "We've got a few folks out with injuries, but Medical assures me they'll all be back to work in a day or two."

"Excellent. Miriam, what's the word from the passengers?"

"Confusion and fear, Admiral. Knowing that we're in good shape will bring a lot of relief to the passengers. On the bright side, our cleanup volunteers enjoyed themselves, and have been doing a fine job of putting folks' minds at rest."

"Good to know. Please convey our gratitude for the help. Their willingness to lend a hand has sped up our recovery efforts immensely. Now, as soon as we're ready, we'll rejoin the galaxy and see what we can find on this arm of the big wheel of stars.

"So, if there's nothing further ..."

"Actually, Admiral ..."

"Sheila?"

"Security would like to bring something before the senior staff for consideration. This is the brainchild of Ensign Hal White, and I have to admit, I do agree with his assessment."

Jeannie sat back down, smiling. "Proceed."

"I'd rather let Hal explain it himself, it's his idea."

"All right, Sheila, so be it." Jeannie smiled and reached for her comm. "Ensign Hal White to the bridge briefing room, repeat, Ensign Hal White to the bridge briefing room."

"On my way."

He arrived shortly and stood waiting. Jeannie nodded and indicated he should sit. "Hal, Sheila tells us you've hatched a plan you'd like to share with us. Let's hear it."

"Thank you, Admiral, Commander Singh. Actually, this is the work of several people. We learned on our last exploratory mission that things can go dangerously awry. As a result of that misadventure, we have new and far more effective armor. However, I believe that's just the first step.

"We have an explorer ship, two salvage ships, and two multi-function ships. Admiral, I believe we need a specialized ship for those occasions when things go wrong."

"What sort of ship do you have in mind, Hal?" asked Jeannie.

"I'd like to see a tough ship, like the new EX2 or one of the Earalith scout ships. I'd like to see her crewed with a two-fold purpose, crew survival and recovery, and medical."

Jeannie smiled and leaned her elbows on the table. "Elaborate."

"Well, since the troubles on Stormy, SUVI 20 has been working with a few of the older passengers and SUVI hunters, developing a training course designed to greatly improve chances for survival in case of being temporarily stranded on a planet. She's learning and teaching how to make fire, hunt and kill food, find edible plants, find and/ or make shelter, and how to create signals that will make it easier to locate a stranded crewman.

"Jake and I have been teaching combat training to those same volunteers as well. Sessas and Lilly have taught basic botany, how to locate a food source, and our Chief Medical Officer has, in her spare time, been teaching basic first aid. Twenty has also, with Harlan's assistance, developed a planetary survival kit that everyone should wear if they're going groundside.

"Admiral, if you think this is a good idea, there's a crew ready to man whatever ship you choose."

Jeannie looked at the people gathered around and could see they liked the idea. "So, the idea here is to have an emergency response ship manned with a specially trained crew, a crew ready for anything and everything. Is that right?"

"That's it, Admiral. What do you think?"

"I like it, Hal. What do you think, Carla?"

"I like it. It was Twenty's first aid that kept Jake alive on that planet. Mr. Sacumbtu could have benefitted from this training. He and his crew were in bad shape when we got them back."

"Moira?"

"Me? I like it, Jeannie. I can finish EX3 and equip her for the task if you like."

"Sheila?"

"I like it, Admiral. I'd also like to see that ship heavily armed, just as a precaution."

"Brandon?"

"I agree with Sheila. With that kind of ship, we could go in hard and bring our people out quickly. I'd also like to see it equipped with a full medical bay."

Jeannie arched an eyebrow at Moira. "Oh, aye, I can do that Jeannie, but it'll cut back on the number of crew she can carry. Twelve crew, max."

"Hal?"

"Admiral?"

"Does your crew fit that bill?"

"It can, sure, easily. We've got five survivor/infiltrators, four flight crew, and two emergency medics. Everybody is trained on every job, but some are specialized."

Jeannie grinned at him. "So, whose idea got this all started?"

Hal chuckled. "I guess it was mine. I put weapons on Sessas, started teaching Twenty some combat, and talked Jake into getting Harlan to design some specialized equipment for us. Carla loved the idea and joined in."

"So, your crew is ready to go?"

"All they need is a ship and a captain."

Jeannie looked at her first officer. Brandon chuckled and nodded. "I can see what you're thinking, Admiral. Sure, why not?"

"Sheila? What do you think?"

"I've actually seen some of them training, Admiral, even joined in a time or two. They're impressive to say the least."

"I see. Hal, what's your job on this crew?"

"I'm the team leader for the strike force."

"All right, so we're agreed this is a good idea. Who's the captain?"

"We don't have one, Admiral," grinned Hal.

"Want the job?"

"Thank you, Admiral, but I'm not ready for that yet. The places and situations we're likely to be involved in require a cool head and a lot of experience."

Jeannie smiled at her friend. "Any recommendations?"

Hal grinned. "Commander Hoffman or Commander Singh would be my first choice."

Jeannie chuckled as she sat back in her chair. "How about it, Brandon, want your own ship?"

"Thanks, but I'll pass, Admiral. I'm enjoying my job here on the Reacher. Give it to Sheila, she likes a bit of excitement."

"How about it, Sheila, want the ship?"

"Are you serious? Yes, of course you are. First you refuse to let me retire, now I have to command a ship?"

"Come on, Sheila, you know you want to."

Commander Singh grinned with delight as she sat back in her chair. "Yes I do, Admiral, yes I do."

"Then I promote you to the rank of Captain. EX3 is your ship, choose your crew and assign whatever rank you desire to each member."

With a bright smile, the newly appointed Captain Singh turned to Hal. "Commander White, you'll be my first officer, go assemble the crew. We'll meet in Security to fully discuss crew positions. Admiral, may I make a request?"

"Ask."

"Since it will take some time to get EX3 ready, and Captain Drake's new ship is now in service, might I have Friendship Two until EX3 is complete?"

"Done. Take Linsey with you and get introduced to the AI. The ship is yours. Brandon, we need a new Chief of Security."

Commander Hoffman just grinned. "Jake White is next in line."

"So be it. Call him in and promote him. Now, is there anything further? No? Then, meeting adjourned, back to work, people." Jeannie was smiling as she rose and took Amanda by the hand and led her from the room.

Chapter #4

The Infiltrators

The new crew assembled in the security office's main meeting room. Sheila Singh stood and began pacing about, then slowly turned to face them. "All right, you people have been training and preparing as an exercise, something fun to do, for the most part. I've been watching and occasionally participating for the same reasons. The time for that has passed, the Admiral's given us the official blessing, assigned us a ship, and has put me in command.

"So, anyone who isn't wholly committed to this ship, crew, and purpose, please leave this room now." No one moved a muscle. "Excellent. Commander Hal White will now give you your assigned posts aboard the Retriever. Yes, I'm exercising my right as captain to rename our ship, at least among this crew. Commander."

"Thank you, Captain. I'll lead the Strikers who will be the first off the ship. The Strike Force will be me, Rhonda, and Billy, plus our two special consultants, SUVI 20 and Sessas. We're the first responders.

"Flight crew is Orlon on pilot, Ellen is engineer, Tagora is on sensors, and Kumar is on weapons. Forest and Grady are the medics, and Captain Sheila Singh is our captain. All yours, Captain."

"Thank you, Commander. Now, let's go down to the launch bay and introduce ourselves to the AI of Friendship Two. He'll be our ship for the foreseeable future."

Six days of hard practice later, Captain Sheila Singh felt her crew was ready. They were soon about to get their first mission. She smiled with delight as the announcement came over the speakers. "Attention all ship's personnel, the Reacher is ready to set sail. We will be approaching the nearest star in a few hours. All captains, ready your ships and crew."

Jeannie stood on the bridge with her first and second officers. She was smiling. "Brandon, are we ready?"

"Ship is secure and ready to sail, Admiral."

"Emmet, are we set?"

"The bridge is ready, Admiral; course laid in and star drive online."

"Make it happen, Emmet."

"Aye, Admiral. Pilot, engage the star drive."

"Engaging drive, aye." As he threw the switch the Reacher gave a small shudder then vanished from her position just off the galactic arm. Six hours later, she dropped sub-light and slowed as she neared the planetary system. She was instantly bombarded by hails from several ships in several different languages.

"What the ...??? Shields. Captain Linsey da Silva to the bridge, Commander Jake White to the bridge. SUVIs Eighteen and Twenty to the bridge. Sensors, talk to me, are any of those ships making any threatening moves?"

"No, Admiral. They seem to be derelicts for the most part. I'm not getting any reading that would suggest an active propulsion system."

"Thank you, Anita. Emmet, get us stopped as fast as you can."

"Ship all stop, aye. ... Ship has stopped, Admiral."

"Thank you, Emmet. Now ... Ah, Linsey, what do you make of this?"

Linsey tilted her head slightly as she listened to the jabbering coming over the speakers. "Comms, can you isolate a single one of these?"

"One moment, Captain da Silva." The man fussed with his control panel for a moment, then only one voice was heard.

Linsey nodded as she listened for a moment. "I have no idea what it's saying, Admiral, but it's an automated message that keeps repeating. It could be a plea for help or a warning to veer off. Comms, give me another one." He did.

After several more with the same results, Linsey sighed and turned to Jeannie. "They're all automated, Admiral. I have no idea what they're saying."

Jeannie smiled as she nodded. "How can you tell, Linsey?"

"They keep repeating the same phrases with the exact same inflections. A living speaker will always make small changes to inflections even when repeating the same message. These are all exactly the same. We're getting messages from nine different sources, all different languages, and all automated."

"I see, thank you, Linsey." Jeannie turned to the other people she'd called to the bridge. "Eighteen, Twenty, are you getting anything?"

"I sense no immediate danger here, Admiral," replied SUVI 20.

"This is a graveyard," said SUVI 18, her eyes glowing amber. "So many ships, peoples, stranded here, no way to survive. So much fear ..." Linsey reached for her hand and gave it a gentle squeeze. Eighteen smiled weakly and nodded.

"Jake?"

"Security is on full alert, Admiral."

Jeannie nodded as she began to pace. "All right, Emmet, nudge us forward, let's see what happens. Sensors, stay sharp."

"Aye, Admiral."

The Reacher slowly approached a number of alien ships that orbited one of the planets in the goldilocks zone. The messages continued to batter at them, but Linsey was monitoring them and found nothing but automated voices. One ship actually began to turn toward them, albeit slowly. A different message came from the speakers.

"All stop," barked Jeannie.

"All stop, aye," replied the pilot as his hands flew over the controls. The Reacher stopped, but the other continued her slow rotation until she was facing the Reacher fully.

"Linsey?"

"Working, Admiral." She was fussing with a devise in her hand that was connected to her head with an earpiece.

"We've been working on a translation device, Admiral," smiled Eighteen. "If it works properly it should help Linsey to decipher some of this more quickly."

"What about you, Eighteen?"

"I sense no immediate danger from that ship. Twenty?"

"I get nothing," was the soft reply.

"Hmm. Options, opinions, people."

"I'd say that ship is moving on thrusters only," replied Brandon. "If that's true, then it still has some functioning systems online. I'm hoping weapons isn't one of them, but I wouldn't count on it."

"Second that," muttered Jake.

"Agreed," mused Jeannie. "Linsey?"

"All I can give you is an educated guess, Admiral. I believe the message coming from that ship is a plea for help. I base this on the fact the voice isn't sounding threatening, or commanding, but rather trying to remain calm as it speaks. I believe someone recorded that message then put it in a permanent loop. However, I have no way to confirm that."

"Understood. Eighteen, Twenty?"

"I believe Linsey's right about this, Admiral," replied Eighteen.

"As do I. Anita, are they making any threatening moves?"

"None, Admiral. I see no signs of main engine activity and I detect no life forms or movement aboard that ship."

"I see. Recommendations people?"

"I think Retriever should take a closer look, Admiral," grinned SUVI 20.

"Then you'd better get back to your ship," smiled Jeannie as she reached for her comms. "Captain Singh, man your ship and prepare to investigate the facing vessel. Bridge will send you coordinates. Captain Drake, take a look at the planet below, but don't attempt to land as yet; just look her over then come home. Captains, be extremely wary, take no chances."

"Understood, Admiral," came the two responses. A moment later EX2 launched, and Retriever followed.

* * * * *

The scout ship Retriever carefully approached the huge ship that remained facing Reacher. It was nearly as big. The crew of the small ship were all excited and alert as they slowly circled and scanned the stranger, but it made no threatening moves at all. Still, the message continued to broadcast over the comm system.

"Captain?"

"First Officer?"

"I think that's an open port up ahead, are we going in?"

"Absolutely, ready your team."

"Ma'am." With a wide grin Hal White nodded to his advance team and they hurried into spacesuits. They were ready at the rear hatch as Retriever crept through the open port on the big ship. Once they were fully inside the lights came up, exposing a large hangar bay containing hundreds of small ships less than a third the size of the Retriever. No sign of animated movement was found.

"Sensors, anything moving?"

"No life signs anywhere, Captain."

"What can you tell me about those small ships?"

"Not too sure, Captain, but I believe they're heavily armed."

"Pilot, set us down. Commander White, take your team and check out one of those ships. Be careful, don't mess with the controls, just have a close look."

"Aye, Captain." Hal led his team into the airlock and sealed it. The outside hatch hissed open, and they stepped out. "Artificial gravity in evidence, Retriever. Approaching alien ship now. Ship is sealed and, ah, there we go. I have the ship open, looks like a two-man vehicle, the seats appear to be about the right size for a human, instrument panel is unintelligible, but there's something I recognize."

"What is it, Hal? What have you got?"

"It's a hand grip with a trigger mechanism, Captain. I'd say the sensors were right, these ships appeared to be armed. Gripping the handle now, display with cross-hair sights has come live."

"Hal, step away from the weapons."

Sheila Singh chuckled as he responded. "Yes ma'am. Stepping back. Okay, poking around, this looks like ammo stores, food locker, equipment of some sort, and a bonanza."

"Hal?"

"Looks like the pilot's personal locker, a few articles of clothing, a couple of trinkets, and what looks like an info tablet. Could this be useful to Captain da Silva?"

"Quite possibly. Bring it with you and return to Retriever, we'll explore further."

They returned and stripped off the enviro suits. Hal put the tablet in the storage compartment as the captain gave orders to move on slowly. Retriever fairly crept along the seemingly endless corridor of small fighter ships. "Hal, do you notice anything unusual here?"

"Aye, Captain. There seems to be a lot of empty stalls at this end. The big question here is, where are they?"

"That was my thought," said the captain. "Comms, contact the Reacher.

"Aye, Captain. This is Retriever calling Reacher. Reacher, do you copy?"

"Reacher here, Sorenson commanding. What have you found, Sheila?"

"This is definitely a warship, Admiral, lined from stem to stern with small two-man fighters. The thing is, there are a number of small ships missing. We found no signs of life as yet. Continuing to explore."

"Sounds good. I'll warn Explorer to keep an eye out for those small fighters. Did you find anything Linsey might use to help with the language?"

"We have a small info tablet; we'll transport it over."

"Thank you, Retriever. Good hunting; stay in touch. Reacher out."

"The tablet has been transported, Captain."

"Thank you, Hal. Sensors, any signs of life yet?"

"No, ma'am, nothing yet, but I'm detecting another passageway twenty meters ahead."

"Will the ship fit through?"

"No, Captain."

"Set us down, Pilot. Looks like you're up again, Hal."

"Yes, Captain. Suit up, team, let's see what we can do to map this beast."

They set out toward the doorway to the passage. It silently slid open to let them pass. Once they had cleared the opening the door slid closed behind them. Rhonda turned and stepped close to the door which obligingly slid open again. With a nod of approval, she turned back to follow her team.

Up ahead, Hal was checking his instruments. He nodded and cautiously opened the faceplate on his suit and took a sniff of the air. He quickly closed it again. "Hal, report."

"Aye, Captain. We've entered the main ship, it still has atmosphere, stinks like hell so we're keeping the suits on for now. No signs of life anywhere so far."

"Very good. Carry on, Commander."

They soon reached a divide in the corridor. "Rhonda, Twenty, Billy, go right, thirty meters only then check in. Sessas, you and I will go left." She nodded that she understood then led the way with Hal close behind.

They continued on until the corridor took a sharp left turn then ended at what looked like doors. Hal stepped close and they opened to a small boxlike room. "Looks like elevators. Hal to Retriever. Looks like we found some elevators. Can't read the instructions. Sending visuals now."

Sheila was watching the screen. "Visuals received, Hal. Return to SUVI 20, she's found something interesting."

"On my way."

Hal and Sessas swiftly returned to the junction, then onward to find Rhonda waiting by another set of elevators. Rhonda grinned and opened the lift doors. "It's up here."

The machine rose smoothly then stopped. They stepped out to see SUVI 20 and Billy wandering along a row of strange looking transparent tubes. "So, what's all this?" asked Hal.

"Assholes," replied Sessas, peering into one of the beds, the translation device on her tunic easily translating her words.

"She's right, Hal," agreed Twenty, as she joined them. "Every one of these looks like a cryo bed with a body inside. I think we've found the crew."

"Wow. Sessas, what makes you call them enemies?"

"All hold weapons, Hal. Not need for sleep."

"Makes sense to me. We should ..."

"Ship to Commander White, respond."

"Here, Captain."

"You're three decks up, what have you found?"

"Looks like cryo beds with bodies inside. No signs of anybody awake yet."

"Your suits must be running low on air by now, return to the ship for a recharge."

"On our way."

Hal led the way back and, once inside Retriever, they quickly shed their atmo suits and breathed deeply. Sheila turned to the pilot. "Take us back out to open space, Orlon."

"Open space, aye." The small ship lifted up, turned, and headed back toward the open doors. Once in space she contacted the Reacher.

"Reacher here, Retriever, Sorenson commanding. You find anything interesting?"

"We did, Admiral. First, this thing is a war ship, carrying hundreds, maybe more, small two-man fighters. Second, we found what looks like the crew, all in cryo beds."

"Understood, Sheila, return to Reacher."

"Coming home. Retriever out."

"Why did she call us back?" asked Hal.

"Think about it, Hal. We know that thing is a war ship, so, that tells us those people are unlikely to be friendly. Do we wake them up and face a potential battle, or do we leave them as they are? Those are only two of the many questions Suvi-jean will have to decide." Sheila sighed and leaned back against the rail. "Don't want her job, especially not today."

"Yeah, second that. I wonder how Amanda is doing?"

"I guess we'll soon find out, EX2 is right on our tail," chuckled Rhonda, who was standing at sensors. A few moments later Retriever swept into the landing bay of the Reacher with EX2 close behind.

Chapter #5

Questions

The admiral called for a full senior staff meeting as soon as both ships were back aboard the Reacher. As she hurried toward the bridge, Sheila saw her lover in the corridor ahead. He saw her then turned away. She gave no indication she had noticed, but SUVI 20 had seen it and sighed. She could feel her captain's pain.

Sheila arrived in the briefing room and took her seat while the admiral continued to pace about. "All senior staff and ship's captains present, Admiral," said the first officer.

Suvi-jean stopped pacing and took her seat beside Amanda. "Thank you, Brandon. All right, people, let's have it. Amanda?"

Captain Drake smiled as she spoke. "EX2 went down for a quick look at the planet. The ship performed above expectation, we found no signs of life, but we did find thousands of ships in various stages of damage. Every ship that we saw looked like it had been shot down and it looks like they've been there for a long time."

"Thank you, Captain Drake," smiled Suvi-jean, as she gave Amanda's hand a gentle squeeze. "Sheila?"

"Admiral, we approached the facing ship, looked her over from outside, then found an open cargo bay. We went inside where we discovered hundreds of small two-man fighter ships. At length we found that a fair number were missing.

"Our incursion team checked out the small ships and brought back a tablet which was transported to Reacher. We then found an access corridor which the team explored. There they found the alien crew, probably the fighter crews, all in cryo pods, all with weapons in hand. We then reported in and returned to Reacher."

"So, there you have it people. Brandon, your conclusions?"

"Well, Admiral, I like to err on the side of caution. If that thing is a warship and fully manned, I wouldn't be in a hurry to wake them up.

By the sounds of it they have us thoroughly out gunned. Chances are that could go astray really fast."

"I must agree with you there. Jake?"

"Me?"

"You, Chief of Security. Your assessment please."

"I'm with Commander Hoffman on this one. I wouldn't try to wake them up. I'd say our best bet is to abandon this system and move further in. This place seems to be nothing more than a graveyard for ships caught in that space/time rift like we were."

"Aye," spoke up the chief engineer, "but we used up a bunch of our resources to repair the damage of the rift journey. A graveyard of ships could render up a lot of useful material."

"Now wait," put in Captain Baris, "what are we talking about here? Are we planning to just loot whatever we want from these ships? Are we now to become thieves in the night?"

Jeannie sighed as she turned to face him. "What we are, Grandfather, is the last of a species, several in point of fact. We have no home planet, no empire to support and supply us, we're on our own. We're nomads, scavengers, doing whatever we must to survive and grow strong again. Grandfather, of necessity we must become opportunists and, as Moira has pointed out, opportunity is knocking at our door.

"Sheila, are you certain the whole crew over there is in cryo sleep?"

"No, Admiral. It could take days, perhaps weeks to explore that whole ship. For all we know there could be dozens of them hidden on any one of those decks."

"I see. Linsey, are you making any headway with that language?"

"Some, Admiral. That universal translation program Eighteen and I developed seems to work well. The tablet brought to us from the ship was the personal journal of a pilot. It recorded his kills and the joy he took therein. Definitely not a friendly sort. I'd like to have a go at that ship's bridge, see if I can find the captain's log, learn more about them as a people."

"What of those small fighters?" asked Jake. "Could we learn to use those, keep a couple for Security to use if necessary? Maybe put a couple on each of the small ships and a dozen on the Reacher?"

"An interesting possibility, to be sure, however, let's not get ahead of ourselves. That ship has a crew aboard, therefore it's not salvage. Personally, I'd prefer to leave sleeping aliens lie where they are, at least for the moment.

"Captain Drake, you saw no signs of life down there?"

"None at all."

"All right, catch a rest period then go back down. Olga, take your ship and accompany EX2, see if you can find useful things to bring home for Moira to play with. Sheila, get some sleep then take an extra security detail with you and see what else you can learn from that ship. Try not to disturb anything unless you have to, but learn what you can."

"Admiral, I'd like to go with them, see if I can learn more about these people."

"All right, Linsey, but be careful, take no chances. This is an exploratory mission, people, nothing more."

"Aye, Admiral."

As everyone filed out, Captain Baris remained behind. "Are you going to chew me out again, Grandfather?"

He chuckled at that. "No, Jeannie. I just wanted to thank you for reminding me how much has changed. You're right, we have no home to go to, no empire to supply us. We need to rely on ourselves, become scavengers, survivors, just like our distant ancestors.

"However, I am a bit surprised that you sent Sheila back to that ship, and let Linsey go with her."

"Yeah. In truth I was tempted to send Eamon too, but I can't trust him not to start waking them up. I'm hoping Linsey can learn to read their tech manuals better. Every bit we can learn to advance our technology will help us survive in the long term.

"If those people were awake, I'd offer to trade with them, but since they're not ..."

"Your Viking ancestor says to loot their ship while they're asleep?"

Jeannie laughed at that. "Yes, something along those lines. Grandfather, I have to keep everybody alive if possible. Anything we can learn or gather that will help is a bonus. Yes, my SUVI instincts say run away, avoid any possible conflict, but you saw Emmet's face as well as I did. We're not in great shape for a long flight."

"Yes, I did notice that. You're right, Jeannie, if there's nothing else alive here, except those sleeping warriors, then we should gather what we can, while we can."

Chapter #6

Back to the Ship

Next morning, Retriever returned to the facing ship with extra security, plus Linsey and Eighteen, aboard. Sensors recorded nothing new or unusual, so they went inside and landed near the corridor entry again. This time they tried the elevators Hal had discovered. They went up one floor then stopped and got out.

Linsey and Eighteen were with Hal's strike team, the extra security remaining back with the ship. The corridor was long, with many doorways leading off on either side. Eventually they found the crew quarters, where they gathered a few more personal recording devices, but nothing more of use.

Beyond that they found what must have been a training area, further on was the main mess hall, then what could have been an entertainment area, but still nothing of real value. Eventually they came to more elevators.

They went up a floor. Here they found the hydroponics area, long since overgrown then when no further nutrients were available, dead and withered plants were all that was left. It had been that way for a very long time. The medical bay was also on that floor, but again, it had seen no use for a long time.

"Captain to Commander White."

"Here, Captain."

"Your suits must be running low. We've got you on sensors, prepare to be transported back to the ship for a rest and recharge."

"Ready to transport, Retriever."

They all arrived in a flash of light and began to shed their atmo suits. The suits were plugged in to recharge while the crew relaxed with a meal. Sheila caught SUVI 18 gazing at her sadly. "Something on your mind, Eighteen?"

"It'll keep, Captain."

Sheila sighed and let her shoulders slump. "It's all right, Eighteen, I'm okay." Eighteen nodded and returned her attention to her meal. Now Hal was gazing at her. "Something wrong, Commander?"

"No, ma'am."

"Is there no damn way at all to keep a secret on this ship?"

"It's none of our business, Captain."

"No, it isn't, but I can see it's messing with morale, so here it is. Yes, I'll admit I'm a bit distracted, it's a personal issue, I can deal with it myself. The big problem here is we're on an explore mission, not a rescue mission. The enforced inactivity is making me a bit crazy and giving me too much time to ruminate on my personal life instead of the task at hand."

"There's an easy fix for that," grinned Linsey.

"Oh? Do tell, Captain da Silva."

"This is a big ship to explore, and we have enough people to make up a second exploration crew, leave me here to work on these tablets and you go exploring."

"Leave you here?"

"I hold captain's rank; I can babysit a stationary ship easily enough."

Sheila chuckled at that. "Maybe you're right, Linsey, I do need to see some action. All right, we catch a short sleep cycle then I'll take the extra security people and go poking around, Hal and his team can continue searching for the bridge, and you can babysit." There was a round of chuckles at that.

Soon after the sleep cycle they were ready to go. Hal led his people up one level from where they left off. Sheila and her crew were transported to where Hal and crew ended the day before. They set out cautiously but found nothing of great interest.

"Captain to Commander White."

"Here Captain."

"Anything interesting?"

"More empty crew quarters, an extensive brig with a number of cadavers, big storage areas, mostly empty, but that's all. We're about to go up a floor."

"Carry on then. We found nothing useful here. We're going back down to see if we can find engineering. That should be close to the main bay."

"Understood, Captain."

With that he was gone, and she led her people back to the elevators. They rode down to the main floor then went to the bank of elevators that led to the cryo beds. Sheila wanted to see them for herself. She took her time wandering among the tubes then sighed. "Notice anything, people?"

"Nothing's moving, Captain."

"Not what I meant, Ellen."

"Oh, you meant that barely half the cryo tubes seem to be functioning?"

"Yes, that would be it."

"Ah-huh, I had noticed that. Captain Singh, there's another entryway over there."

Sheila turned and spotted the open doorway, a chill running up her spine. "That wasn't open a moment ago."

"Well, it's open now. Sound off, people." They did. "All present, Captain," said Ellen Brady. "It wasn't one of us who opened it. Maybe it was on auto, or a glitch, or something else."

"My bet is on something, or somebody, else," replied Sheila. "Close in, people. Captain to Commander White."

"Here, Captain."

"Stay sharp, we may not be the only ones awake here."

"Understood."

"Okay, people, let's go see if we can find who opened the door." With that, Sheila led them over to the doorway, took a quick look through, but saw nothing, just another empty corridor. Cautiously, she led them through. As soon as the last one cleared the door it slammed shut with a whoosh. They all spun around, and one man tried to reopen it, but to no avail.

"Ah well, if we can't go back, then we must go forward." Sheila turned and led them down the passageway.

They soon came to another door that led to a room full of technical equipment. Several screens were active, showing multiple readouts, but without the language there was no way for them to understand what they were seeing.

"Captain to Retriever."

"Retriever here, da Silva commanding."

"Linsey, are you making any headway with that language yet?"

"It's a lot simpler than Earalith, so we're getting there. I can have a translator pad ready for you in a couple of hours."

"Excellent. Transport us back to the ship and we can recharge our suits while you work on that."

"Roger that." Linsey pointed at the man standing at the transport controls. A few failed tries later he shook his head sadly.

"Ship to Captain Singh, that's a negative on the transport. Something seems to be blocking the beam."

"Understood, we'll find another way back. Singh out." She looked at her team, men and women she'd worked with for many years. "So, whose idea was it to go exploring again?" There was a round of nervous laughter at that.

"Captain, what will we do if we can't get back?"

"Relax, we'll find our way back. The only thing stopping us is a door, and a laser drill will make short work of that if it comes to it. I'd just rather not do that if we can find another way. We don't want to disturb anything unless we have to. Come on, let's see what else we can find."

They continued down the corridor to another elevator. "Why not?" said Sheila as the doors opened. They squeezed inside and the machine dropped swiftly to open into a room cold as space, and just as dark. As they stepped out, dim light came on showing them what could only be the engine room.

"Looks like the engine room to me," said a voice behind her.

Sheila had to agree. "Yes, and by the looks of things, these engines are done. This ship isn't going anywhere any time soon. I'll bet they put everybody to sleep when they realized there was no hope for the ship. They're waiting for a rescue ship to come for them."

"Yep, this ship has been here a long time, so now comes the big question," he replied.

"Who locked the door behind us?"

"That's the one, Captain, that and who turned on the lights when we got here?"

"Good questions, every one," chuckled Sheila. "Sadly, I have no answers, just more questions."

"I've got the answer to a question," said another of the team.

"Oh? Which question would that be?"

"What do they look like outside those frosted cryo beds? I've got corpses over here."

Sheila and the others swiftly approached her position to find her gazing at several dismembered bodies, badly burned. A careful look around told the story. There'd been an explosion in the engine room, crippling the ship and killing several of the crew as well as blowing a hole in the hull.

"The ship has still got auxiliary power, but it's not getting it from here. There's got to be another power source nearby somewhere. Spread out and search but stay within visual contact."

Several voices answered her order with an "Aye, Captain," as they separated and began the search.

The search turned up nothing, so they returned to the elevator and went back up to the original floor. "Captain, my suit's almost out of air."

"As is mine," replied Sheila. "Let's see if we can transport out of here now." The answer was no.

"Da Silva to Captain Singh."

"Here, Linsey."

"Hal tells me you won't like it, but the atmosphere is breathable, Captain. Your suits are running low, but you can breathe without them. Return to the room where the cryo beds are, or as close as you can get, help is on the way."

"Acknowledged. Okay, let's try that door again." She led them back to the door and this time it opened at her approach. They retraced their steps to the ship without incident and found Hal and company gearing up to go for them, laser drills in hand.

Sheila sighed with relief as she removed her helmet and drew a deep breath of fresh air. "Damn, that was close. Hal, report."

"Nothing exciting on our end, Captain. We covered two more floors, found a couple of maintenance areas, sleeping quarters, another mess hall and kitchen, plus what looked like an infirmary. No signs of life and nothing of great interest."

"Good to know. On the other hand, we had our adventures. First we found another door leading from the cryo room, went through, and it locked behind us. Something also blocked the transporters from reaching us. We moved on to find more elevators and rode down to the main engine room. There we learned they'd had an explosion that killed a number of them and blew a hole in the hull.

That area was sealed off, but something wanted us to find it, to see what had happened to them. Once we'd explored that area we returned and the doorway to the cryo room opened again allowing us to return."

"Okay, so somebody else is awake on this ship, and they wanted you to find the engine room. Why?"

"No idea," Sheila replied with a sigh of fatigue. "Twenty, is that magic intuition of yours picking up anything?"

"Not really, Captain. I get the sense that someone's awake all right, but I sense no harm or ill intent. Eighteen?"

"I get a mix of emotions, sorrow, fear, resignation, mourning, and faint hope. There is a lot of death surrounding this ship, and many dead inside it."

Linsey reached out to take her hand. "Easy, sweetheart, I've got what I need now, we can go home. I can make a translation device that will help our explorers."

"I heard that," said Sheila. "Comms, get me the Reacher."

"Reacher, aye. Retriever calling Reacher, come in Reacher."

"Sorenson here, Retriever."

"Admiral, Linsey says she has what she needs to make a translation device for us. I'd like to return until that's ready. We've had our adventures today."

"Come home, Retriever, you can tell us all about it when you get here."

"On our way."

At Captain Singh's nod the pilot set to work, the ship rose up, turned about, then flew out of the big ship to return to Reacher. A short while later, while Linsey was working on the device, Captain Sheila Singh sat giving her report to the senior staff.

"So, you believe someone, or something, deliberately led you to the engine room to show you the devastation there?"

"I do, Admiral."

"I see. If this is true, then perhaps it was showing you that the ship is no threat but needing help. However, if that were the case, then why not make direct contact? There is much more to be discovered here. Once Linsey has the device ready, go back and see what more you can learn.

"Sheila, be extremely careful."

"I will, Jeanie, I will."

"Get some rest while you can. I'll let you know the instant Linsey has the device ready for you."

The meeting broke up and Sheila returned to her quarters, Marcus was gone and so was everything he owned. The place seemed eerily quiet. The least he could have done was wait until she returned to say he was leaving, had the courage to face her. She stomped her foot in frustration then returned to Retriever where she settled into one of the sleeping stalls.

* * * * *

While Captain Sheila Singh and crew caught a sleep cycle, a single body shed a stealth suit and sighed. Ka'Ron knew that his life sign would now be detected on the newcomer, but it couldn't be helped, the suit was failing anyway. Casting it aside, he sank into the captain's chair and nodded off to sleep.

* * * * *

While the crew of Retriever and the mystery man on the alien ship all rested, the crew of EX2 settled down to a meal of rations. The ship had returned to a standard orbit. "Thirteen, your assessment?"

"Well, Captain, it's obvious every ship we found has been in a battle and lost. The thing is, some seem to be a lot older than others, like this battle has been going on for a long time."

"That was my thought as well. Let me speculate a bit here. Whatever tossed us across the galaxy has been at this for a long time, randomly throwing ships into this area. Somewhere it picked up a serious warship and dropped it off. That ship attacked and destroyed everything it encountered.

"However, that would suggest the people on said warship are nearly immortal, for the timeline here is pretty long by our standards. Your thoughts, people?"

"I'd say you've got a pretty good picture of it, Captain," replied SUVI 3. "Thirteen?"

"Agreed. You're an engineer, Three, any idea how they could remain active for so long?"

"Cryo sleep would be my guess," she replied. "A new ship gets dropped off, our warship awakens it's crew automatically, they realize the newcomer isn't one of their own, so they attack."

"That makes sense," agreed Amanda. "By the looks of those downed fighters the last group they attacked put up one hell of a fight. I'll bet those dead fighters are the ones missing from the big ship.

"So, to the next step. There's plenty of salvage here, do we give Recovery the go ahead?"

Thirteen chuckled then spoke. "Your decision, Captain, but I'd say it's a go."

"Yeah, that was my thought." Amanda reached for her comm unit. "EX2 to Recovery."

"Olga here, Amanda. What's the good word?"

"I say you're clear to go. EX2 will remain above you in orbit. We'll let you know the instant anything comes this way that shouldn't."

"You're riding shotgun?"

"Yep, you folks hunt and gather, and we'll watch your back."

"Acknowledged with thanks. Recovery out."

Amanda turned back to her crew. "All right, people, we'll work in shifts, half of us awake and on alert status while the rest grab some sleep. First shift, me on pilot, Thirteen on weapons, Lilly on sensors, and Ray on comms monitoring all frequencies. The rest of you get some sleep."

Chapter #7

Retriever Returns

Sheila Singh entered the mess looking like she hadn't slept at all. The place was busy, busier than she would have liked, but the idea of another meal of rations was even less appealing. She chose a plateful then looked around for a space to sit. There, at the far end of a long table, sat a lone Earalith woman.

"Hi, mind if I join you?" asked Sheila as she sat down facing the woman.

"It appears you already have," said the woman, a gentle smile on her lips. "No, I don't mind. My name is Ernel, and you are Captain Sheila Singh."

"Guilty as charged," replied Sheila, smiling at last. "I've met most of the Earalith before, but somehow we've missed each other."

Ernel's smile broadened. "It wasn't deliberate, Captain, at least not on my part."

Sheila laughed heartily at that. "Nor was it on mine, Ernel. Thank you for that, I did need a laugh. Call me Sheila, it sounds friendlier than Captain."

"Thank you, Sheila. Is the captain designation fairly new?"

"It is, could you tell?"

"You seem a bit stressed."

"I am, for a number of reasons."

"Sorry, I didn't mean to pry."

"You didn't, Ernel, you met a new friend and showed an interest and compassion for that person. I took no offense."

"Good, for none was meant. So, we're friends now? I'd like that, Sheila, for I have few friends and I miss that. Every friend I had was killed centuries ago."

Sheila sighed and gave the woman a gentle smile. "I can't begin to imagine how hard that must be for you."

"Thank you for that. So few understand; I lost the love of my life then. He and I were inseparable, joined at the hip as you people say, madly in love. We perished together, but I was recalled from the shores of death. My beloved wasn't, and I can't seem to get past the mourning of him.

"Antha tells me to make friends, that sharing time with people will help me through the process. It's been many months now, but I've made little progress in that department."

"It takes time, Ernel, trust me. Take it at your own pace."

"That sounds like experience talking."

"It is," sighed Sheila. "I lost the love of my life just before the Reacher first set sail many years ago. Yes, I've had a few lovers since that time, but they all seem to drift away."

"One just recently?"

"That easy to read, am I?"

"Forgive me, Sheila, I didn't mean to pry."

"No, it's fine, Ernel. The man was younger, stronger, but nowhere near my skill level, yet for some reason he insisted on training with me. It got quite competitive between us, and the man didn't like losing. I got home yesterday to find our quarters empty."

"Ouch."

"Yes, well, it's an old story. Ernel, thanks for listening. Sadly, I must get back to work now. Shall we meet again when I get back?"

"I'd like that, Sheila, I enjoyed our chat over a meal. I'll keep watch for your ship."

* * * * *

The nagging sound of the proximity alarm dragged Ka'Ron from a deep sleep. Good, the explorers were returning, there was still a chance. Doing his best to ignore the pain in his body, he ate a small stale ration, the last he had, smoothed out his fur as best he could, and then stood to the screen. Yes, they were inside again. He smiled as he brushed the fur back from his eyes then threw the switch to block their usual entry. "You will have to search for it, but it is there, you can find it. You have to find it."

As he watched them on monitors, he leaned heavily against the consol. Ka'Ron had been trapped on that bridge for what must have been long ages. He and his team had penetrated the killer ship and made their way to the bridge, the second team had reached the engine room, but got caught in the blast as they sabotaged it.

That blast had done its job, crippling the monster, but it had trapped Ka'Ron's team. They'd won the firefight with the bridge crew but were unable to escape. They managed to figure out the controls and put themselves into cryo sleep, but the alien cryo beds were different, and the results were predictable.

Much of the killer ship was on auto, and each time a new ship appeared it awakened the fighters who attacked and destroyed the newcomers then returned to their cryo beds. The same alarms also awakened Ka'Ron and his men, but slowly, over time, they failed until only he was left.

Ka'Ron spent much of his time in cryo sleep now as the food and water were nearly gone and the air was tainted. These new explorers were his last hope, he dare not trust the cryo sleep again. The big problem now was the fighters. If the explorers awakened them, they would be killed, and his last hope would die with them.

* * * * *

Retriever settled gently to the big ship's deck, then the two crews stepped out in full atmo suits. They approached the door to the ship's interior, but it wouldn't open. After several futile attempts, they began to spread out, searching for another entry. It took most of the day, but SUVI 20 finally found it.

As the door slid open and she stepped inside, the lights came up. Hal and the others were close behind her as she entered a room full of some kind of equipment. "Hal to Captain Singh."

"Here. Find anything?"

"We found another way in, Captain. Right now we're in what looks like a control room."

"Don't mess with anything, just see if you can go deeper into the ship. We'll wait for Linsey to crack the language before we start playing with the settings."

"Understood," chuckled Hal, as he nodded to the others. They spread out, looking for further access to the ship. They found it just as their suits began to beep that they were running out of air. The captain recalled everyone to the ship, and they went gladly. The air in that big warship was truly foul.

"Okay, everybody here?"

"All crew returned, and ship sealed up, Captain."

"Thank you, Hal. So, we had no luck at all, but you did. Did you manage to find further access to the ship?"

"We did, Captain, but didn't have time to explore much."

"All right, people, what do you think is going on here? Twenty?"

"Somebody else is awake on this ship, this we suspected. He guided us to the engine room to let us know the ship is badly wounded and not going anywhere, can't maneuver with any speed, and therefore is unlikely to be a threat to Reacher."

"That was my assessment as well," said Sheila. "Are you getting anything at all about our mystery man?"

"I sense no ill intent, but I still feel like we're being manipulated. I think there's something he wants us to find, something he needs us to know."

"Any idea what that might be?"

"None, Captain. None at all."

Sheila nodded and seemed lost in thought for a moment. "All right, people, options, opinions?"

Hal chuckled as he expressed the desire of the whole crew. "I think we should explore further, Captain."

"As do I, but I'd really like to have access to their language if Linsey could manage it. Comms, get me Captain da Silva."

"Retriever to Captain da Silva, Retriever calling Captain da Silva."

"Friendship here, da Silva commanding. How can I be of service?"

"Sheila here, Linsey. Have you made any headway with that language yet?"

"I think I've got it. We're on our way over to try out my new invention. Be right there."

A few moments later Friendship landed lightly beside Retriever. They locked up and Linsey crossed over with Eighteen close behind, carrying a box of some kind. "Hi there, intrepid explorers," grinned Linsey. "This magical machine should be able to manage the language, both sound and written symbol. Want to test it out?"

"Love to," replied Sheila. "How does it work?"

"The camera is here, and with luck the program will translate it onto this screen."

"My suit's all recharged, shall I go test it?" suggested Hal.

His captain gave him the nod. "Go for it."

Hal and his team suited up again and he carried the box to the door that had refused to open before. He held the camera up to the text above the door and a moment later the screen came alive. "To open door manually press at lock and slide door open."

"Wow, that is so cool," exclaimed Hal. "Sadly, it's not working."

"Hal, what's the problem?" asked Linsey. "What do you see?"

"The machine says to press on the door and slide it open, but it's not working."

"So, what you're telling me is my invention worked, but the door is stuck, is that right?"

His laughter was easy to hear. "Yes, that's what I'm saying. Your translator is working fine, but the damn door isn't."

"Then my work here is done," grinned Linsey. "We have to get back to Reacher, Recovery One has brought us a wealth of stuff to explore.

Have fun folks." With that, she and Eighteen returned to Friendship and left.

"Hal?"

"Yes, Captain."

"Go back to that place you found today, see if Linsey's magic machine can make any sense of it?"

"On our way."

They quickly marched to the newly discovered door which obediently opened as they approached. A long time later Sheila's patience ran out. "Retriever to team leader. Hal, what's going on?" She got no response. "Hal, respond." Still nothing. "Sensors, where are they?"

"Gone, Captain. I can't find them anywhere."

"Okay, so, when we were all off the ship could you follow them?"

"Yes, ma'am. Everyone was clearly visible on sensors at that time."

"I see. That tells us they've gone further into the ship and are in a dead zone of some kind. Looks like we'll have to wait for them to come back out." It was a long wait.

"Retriever, do you copy, over?"

"Go ahead, Hal. Are you all right?"

"All good here, Captain, but we're running low on air. Coming home."

"Understood. Pilot, as soon as they're on board, take us back to the Reacher." That didn't happen. As the small ship rose into the air and turned, they discovered the hangar doors had been closed. They were trapped inside the ship.

"Captain, the doors are closed," said Tagora, the Earalith woman on sensors.

"Are you saying we're trapped in here?"

"It appears so, Captain, do we shoot our way out?"

"I doubt that we can. This is a war ship, I'll bet it could withstand anything we could throw at it. Orlon, see if you can contact the Reacher."

"Aye, Captain," replied the pilot. "Retriever calling Reacher, come in Reacher."

"Reacher here, go ahead Retriever."

"The entry point to the ship has been closed," said Sheila. "We're going to look for another way out."

"Understood. Do you need assistance?"

"Not at this time, we'll keep exploring, see if we can find another exit."

"Stay in touch, Retriever. Good hunting. Reacher out."

"So, we're going exploring?"

"Not just yet, Hal. Twenty, give me your take on the situation."

"All right, Captain. As I see it, we've got company on this ship, but for some reason our unknown friend doesn't want to make contact, or he can't. Since we arrived on this ship, it would be obvious that we're smart enough to figure out that it's a war ship, so he let us see the cryo beds believing we wouldn't try to wake them up. All that tells me he has a problem and wants us to help fix it.

"He led you to the engine room to show that the ship is crippled, can't leave the system. For whatever reason he wants us to help him. My guess, and this is just a guess, our friend could be the guy who sabotaged the engine room."

Sheila sighed and leaned back against a panel. "I had considered that. The blast in the engine room was definitely from inside. Now, here's the tricky part. From what we've learned, this ship is nearly as old as the Earalith Empire. How did our friend survive this long?"

"On the other hand, is he just another explorer who got trapped in here and needs our help to get back out?"

"If that last was the case, Captain, why hasn't he tried to contact us directly?"

"Unknown, Twenty, but there could be any number of reasons. Right now, it's all speculation at best. So, here's the reality of our situation, we're trapped, we have no one that we're aware of to rescue, so we're down to survival while we search for a way out.

"Sensors, is there any apparent path to freedom that you can see?"

"Negative, Captain. Nothing useful on sensors."

"Very well then, Grady, how are the supplies? How long can we last in here?"

"Three weeks on reasonable rations, Captain. We'll have to be careful of the water, it'll run out first."

"Understood. People, we've been training for survival on a planet, but that training isn't a lot of good where we are now. So, this is our big test and it's time to get a bit more proactive here and show how adaptable we truly are. Hal, take your team and see if you can find the damned bridge, or at least the control room where we can access the hangar bay doors.

"Comms, see if you can connect me with Captain da Silva and the admiral."

* * * * *

Ka'Ron sighed deeply as he eased himself back into the cryo bed. He dared not close the lid for he might never awaken again, yet he was weary and weak from lack of nutrition. He pulled the lid halfway down until he felt the stab as the feeding tubes attached themselves.

He would sleep and the machine would feed him, or so he hoped. His biggest fear was that the lid might close while he slept. The big bay doors were closed, it was safe to sleep, his guests weren't going anywhere.

Chapter #8

Escape

"Captain Singh, I have the admiral and Captain da Silva for you."

"On screen."

Jeannie's face instantly appeared before her. "Sheila, report."

"We're trapped in here, Jeannie, but we're fine. The thing is, we have an unknown entity on board with us, and he seems to have control. He also seems to be trying to guide us or show us something. We need a way to communicate with this person. We've got Linsey's invention, and it works well as a reader, but we need something more.

"SUVI 20 has speculated that the entity might not be native to this ship, but a saboteur who inadvertently got caught in here and is looking for a way out. Much of the ship is damaged due to time or other influences."

"Okay, so how can we help?"

"I need more than a reader from Linsey. I need some way to broadcast vocalization as well. The hope is to begin a dialogue, and if not, at least let them know we're trying and that we mean no harm. Also, if Twenty's right, the unknown may not understand the language of this ship. Have you cracked any of the others from other ships?"

"I have three more," said Linsey who was standing beside the admiral. "I'll program them into a translation unit like we used for the Earalith ships, then I'll transport it over as soon as it's ready."

"Sheila, if it comes to it, we'll crack that ship open to get you out," said Jeannie.

"Thank you, Admiral. Let's save that as a last resort, I think we need to figure this out on our own if possible."

"Understood. Reacher out."

With a sigh of resignation, Sheila turned back to the sensor screen where Hal and his team were visible. She smiled as she watched him work. He was looking for hidden control panels, using the translator as well as the butt of his blaster to test each wall panel he came to. If there was a hidden passageway or control module anywhere, Hal would find it.

While Hal worked, Sessas and Twenty patrolled, Rhonda and Billy stood guard. Nothing moved or made a sound on the eerily derelict ship.

"It's a bust, Captain," grumbled Hal, as he struggled out of his space suit. "We came up empty."

"It's been a long day, people," replied Sheila. "Linsey's working on something that might help us, so, while she works and we wait, let's have a meal then get some rest. We'll put Ship on auto alert, just in case, then grab some sleep."

They ate a meal of rations then settled into the small bunks as best they could. Several hours later the ship's alarm system awakened them. "Ship?"

"Your wake-up call as requested, Captain."

"Thank you, Ship. Did anything interesting happen while I was asleep?"

"An object was transported in, Captain, and a message. A computerized device and a private message for you."

"A private message? Route it to here, visual only at first." She was expecting to see the face of her lover, but it wasn't from Marcus, it was from Ernel, the Earalith woman she'd met in the mess hall. 'Hello, intrepid explorer. I missed you at lunch today, hope you're having fun and a world of success. I'm also hoping you have lots of exciting stories to tell when you return. Your friend, Ernel.'

With a bemused smile, Sheila responded to the message. "My dear friend, Ernel, at the moment we're trapped inside a derelict ship, boring as hell. Tell you all about it when I get back and we'll celebrate with too many desserts. Sheila." She sent it off then stretched, adjusted her uniform, and stepped out of the small sleeping cubicle.

The crew made a meal of rations, then Hal's team gathered at the hatch. "All right, team, today we're going for the bridge, wherever the hell that might be. Twenty, got your war hammer?" She patted the weapon hanging at her belt. "Good, we may need it. We may have to be a bit more insistent today."

They stepped out and headed for the last place they'd been. They could hear the captain's message being broadcast throughout the ship in three languages they did not understand.

Roughly translated it said, "We mean you no harm, we're here to help. Please respond, let us help you." It kept repeating through the languages.

"Okay, people, here's where we entered the dead zone," said Hal. "From this corridor they can't see us on sensors, nor can they raise us on comms. We went through that door but found nothing of interest. Let's try this one over here."

Hal used the translator and discovered the next room was a control room for the crew cryo beds. "Let's not mess with that right now, we're looking for the bridge." A few more steps into the long corridor brought them to another door. This one only said trophies. He tried the door to no avail.

"Okay, I'm tired of our unseen friend calling all the shots. Twenty, see what you can do with that door."

"Stand back," she grinned. With a dancing step and spin, the long-handled hammer in her hands sped through a wide arc to land at the edge of the door with a loud smack. Obligingly the door buckled inward, and she kicked it aside. What they saw in that room caused her stomach to rebel and Twenty turned away.

Hal stepped inside and gave a long slow whistle. The room was huge, and lined with trophies, strange weapons, heads and partial bodies of dozens of species in transparent sealed containers, and more. His translator struggled, but he gathered these were the remains of defeated enemies, or more likely, conquered species. "You all right, Twenty?"

"Yeah, it just caught me by surprise. There's another door back there, should I check it out?"

"Let's all go; I don't want to chance any of us getting separated from the group, not on this ship."

He led them to the door at the back and it opened at his touch. It led to a smaller room, obviously a dissection area. Twenty swallowed hard then followed him in. Hal poked around with the translator and eventually found where they recorded every species they conquered; each autopsy performed on a new species.

Billy stepped up and attached a small device to the recording station. A few moments later he had it all downloaded. "Got it, Boss. Captain da Silva will love this cache, so will Dr. Reilly."

"Yeah, well, I've seen enough. Let's get out of here and see what else we can find." As they returned to the large trophy room, they found Rhonda and Sessas inspecting the different types of weapons that were displayed there. "What are you guys doing?"

"Checking to see if anything is useful."

"Is it?"

Rhonda chuckled at that. "Danged if I know. Some of the designs are familiar, you know, a gun has a familiar shape no matter what it's supposed to do. Apparently, most species are bipedal, two arms, hands with opposing thumbs, etc."

"Fine, just be careful where you point those things."

"Yes, Boss," grinned Rhonda as she cradled a large weapon in her arms. Sessas had chosen a short spear of some sort, plus something that looked like a blaster. She, too, nodded then Hal led them back out into the corridor.

They proceeded on to the next door. Twenty opened it with her hammer, but there was nothing inside, just an empty room. On to the next one. This one looked like the air processors, they left it undisturbed and moved on.

* * * * *

Ka'Ron was horrified as he watched SUVI 20 use her hammer to open door after door. "No, no, no, you must not do this. Stop, stop, you will awaken the Wrax and we will all die, as will your ship. You must stop." Frantically he began to flip switches to open doors.

"There, explore as you will. Hopefully I will still be alive when you find me. It would have been so much easier if you'd just followed the doors I opened for you. Hopefully you find me still breathing." He threw another switch and then fell back into the chair, exhausted.

* * * * *

Rhonda suddenly heard a squawk on her comm unit and tried to contact the ship. "Retriever, do you read me? Respond. Retriever, do you copy?"

"Retriever here, Rhonda. All of you come home, the big doors just opened."

"Copy that, coming home." Hal grinned as he nodded his agreement, their suits were running low on air. They reached Retriever without incident and as soon as they were on board the ship lifted off and returned to Reacher.

Sheila was last off the ship, having sent the others on to get some rest. She stepped down to find Ernel waiting for her with a bright smile. Somewhat bemused, Sheila returned the smile and approached her.

Ernel's smile broadened as she reached for Sheila. "Allow me to introduce myself properly," she said as she took Sheila's shoulders in her hands. "I'm Ernel, free citizen of the starship Reacher, friend of Captain Singh."

Sheila grinned with delight as she took Ernel by the shoulders and touched their foreheads together. "Namaste, friend Ernel."

Still smiling, Ernel tilted her head slightly to the side with a raised eyebrow. "Thank you, Sheila. Can you tell me what that word means?"

"It means the divine in me sees the divine in you and is nourished. At least that's what my daddy always told me."

"Oh, I like that." Just then the call came out. "All senior staff to the bridge. All captains to the bridge. SUVIs Eighteen and Twenty to the bridge."

"Oh bugger. How about we get together for that dessert-fest as soon as this meeting is over?"

"I'd like that, Sheila. I'll await you in the mess." She was still smiling as she walked away in a different direction while Sheila headed for the bridge.

* * * * *

"We're all here, Admiral."

"Thank you, Brandon. We're here today to assess our situation, people. Moira, tell me good things."

"Well, Admiral, we were hurting for metals. Amanda found us a wealth of new and interesting things, but nothing up to the standards of the Earalith. We were about to give up when she found an Earalith battlecruiser. It was old, nothing alive on him, the AI core was dead, so our salvage crews began to dismantle him.

"As a result, we've upgraded our weapons, repaired Reacher completely, and are back to having enough metal to put EX4 on the books. Right now, EX2 is in service, and EX3 will be soon. As far as Engineering is concerned, we're good to go."

"Now that is welcome news. So, you don't want to hang around and explore more of those old ships for tech and metal?"

"I didn't say that, Jeannie," replied Moira Duncan, matching the twinkle in the admiral's eye with one of her own.

Suvi-jean chuckled and turned to Amanda. "Captain Drake, how goes the exploration of the planet?"

"So far we haven't found any signs of life, Admiral," replied Amanda. "There's a graveyard of ruined ships, but little more of interest. The thing is, most of them look like they were in a battle and lost."

"Okay, Mandy, want to call that one done?"

"Yes, we could. We've been over it three times."

"All right, leave that one to the salvage crews and move over to the second planet in the goldilocks zone, see if there's anything interesting over there.

"Captain Volkov, what news of the salvage operation?"

"Both ships and crews are focusing on the old Earalith ship, Admiral. That seems to be the metal of choice for Engineering. We've got a few days left to get the best of it."

Jeannie nodded thoughtfully. "Brandon, are we good on the Reacher?"

"All's quiet on the Reacher, Admiral. All repair crews have been hard at work and we're back in top shape."

"Good to know. Emmet?"

"Fuel is topped up and all's ready to sail on the bridge, Admiral."

"Excellent. Jake?"

"All quiet at Security, Admiral. Three men have taken early retirement and I have the replacements in training. I need a second in command, but Captain Singh ran off with the two best candidates, so I'm looking through the records for my best chance."

Sheila turned to face him, shaking an admonishing finger. "Oh no you don't, Jake White. Don't you go raiding my crew."

Jake chuckled at that. "Why Captain Singh, the thought never crossed my mind."

"The hell it didn't, I saw that look in your eye."

"Save the family squabble for later, folks," grinned Jeannie. "Carla, Eamon?"

"Medical is quiet, Admiral," smiled Carla. "Eamon's having fun though."

"Eamon?"

"Amanda brought me DNA samples of a dozen different species, Admiral, and Sheila's crew even more. I'll have lots to play with the next time we're interstellar."

Jeannie nodded, smiling at his boyish enthusiasm. "All right, now for the tough one. Sheila, report."

"We've been investigating the one ship that seemed to have some life in it. We've been careful up to recently, and were making progress, but we discovered we had company on board that ship. Someone or something was trying to tell us something. It kept opening and closing doors, jamming our comms, etc., to lead us to certain places.

I have no idea what it's trying to tell us, but we did discover the ship had been sabotaged from within. Yesterday it closed the big bay doors so we couldn't escape. Linsey sent us a device we could use to broadcast messages in a variety of languages, but it didn't seem to help, we got no reply.

"It was about then SUVI 20 ran out of patience and began to use her unique style of negotiation to start opening doors whether they wanted to open or not. Soon after that all the doors opened including the launch bay doors, so we were able to leave."

Jeannie looked thoughtful for a few moments. Amanda gently patted her arm to bring her back to the room. "Sorry. Eighteen, what can you tell me about this?"

"There is a creature on that ship, weak, dying, alone, and afraid. He is unlike the others found in the cryo beds. He fears them, he opened the doors to let you out so you wouldn't trigger an alarm and awaken them. At least, that is my impression."

"Thank you, Eighteen. Twenty?"

"I'm with Eighteen on this one. When I opened that last door, I got a strong sense of fear, then all the doors opened."

"All right, opinions? Options?"

"I think we should go back and find this person, whoever or whatever he is."

"Twenty?"

"Admiral, whatever that creature is, or has done, its actions speak of a desperate cry for help. Yet it remains cautious, and when I started to make a lot of noise, it gave up the game rather than put all of us at risk. I'd like to help it if we can."

"Okay, anybody else?"

It was Jake who spoke up. "Personally, I don't like the idea of poking around in a ship full of warriors. Let sleeping dogs lie, I say."

"Jake has a point. Sheila, your assessment?"

"Jake does have a point. There are hundreds of small fighter ships in that hold, and enough men to pilot them sleeping in the cryo beds. I have no idea how our ships would stand up to theirs, but if they woke up and came at us, I wouldn't give a lot for our chances, there's just too damned many of them.

"Having said that, they're obviously still asleep, and the doors are open. It just seems wrong to leave someone there to die alone."

"Do you want to go back in and look for our mystery man?"

Sheila grinned. "Well, we are supposed to be a rescue ship, right?"

Jeannie chuckled at that. "Emmet, have the bridge sensors noticed any activity on the stranger?"

"No, Admiral. We were able to detect our own people, and one other, but no more."

"All right, aim our new energy cannon right at the facing ship. Go ahead, Sheila, see what you can do, but if you run into trouble, make a break for it and we'll blast them out of the sky. Linsey, have you got anything that can help them in their search?"

"I've been working on a new toy, Admiral. I've programmed every language I can find, human or alien, into it. With a bit of luck, the computer should be able to extrapolate the language and allow you to communicate with who or whatever is talking to you. I can have a few ready by the end of the night shift."

"Make it happen, Linsey. All right, Sheila, you have a go. So, anything else? No, all right, get some rest people. Meeting adjourned."

* * * * *

The meeting had taken longer than expected and Sheila found herself hurrying toward the main crew mess hall. She sighed with relief and a bit of bemusement as she found Ernel there with two plates of desserts. With a grin of mischief Ernel pushed one plate across the table as Sheila sat down. "Wow, this looks like all my favorites."

"Good, for that was my plan."

"Thank you, Ernel. Tell me, what prompted this?"

"You looked a bit stressed when you came off the ship. I thought you could use a boost, so I asked the cooks which desserts you favor."

"That was really sweet of you, thank you."

"My pleasure, now I have something more for you." As she spoke, Ernel pushed a thin wire headpiece across the table.

Sheila gazed at it with a raised eyebrow. "What is this?"

"It is a rare and unusual thing, the first piece of artwork from a well-known artist in hundreds of thousands of years."

"Hundreds of ... you made this?"

"Yes. I was a rather successful artist before I died," she grinned. "You can also plug it in to your wall screen in quarters for a much larger show."

"Really?" said Sheila as she put the delicate headset on and touched the button. Suddenly her vision was of a gentle waterfall surrounded by brightly colored flowers and a variety of birds. The songs of the birds and the gentle sounds of the falling water instantly put Sheila into a relaxed state. She smiled wistfully and sat back for a moment before taking it off.

"Ernel, this is amazing. Did I actually recognize some of that, or am I off base here?"

A bright pleased smile greeted her comment. "Oh, I so hoped you'd recognize a few bits in there. Yes, I checked ship's records, then used a combination of sights and sounds from your early childhood homeland, and those of the planet where you people found me. That was from before the event that killed us, of course.

"You can plug it in and fully surround yourself in it when you're in your quarters."

"Ernel, this is a magnificent gift. I'll requisition new quarters then install this. Thank you."

"You are most welcome, Sheila. New quarters?"

"Yes, I've been sleeping aboard Retriever. The old quarters, where I've spent the last dozen years or more, seem foreign to me now. There's just too much about the place that reminds me of him."

"It wasn't a gentle parting?"

"He just walked away from me, walked away and never once looked back or spoke a word to me." Ernel didn't say anything, just nibbled delicately at the dessert. "He insisted on training with me, but it swiftly became competitive, and the man didn't like losing. I've been the martial arts champion on the Reacher ever since I came aboard, and he knew that."

Ernel nodded, then grinned. "I will never compete with you, Sheila, unless it's for the last piece of this cake, then you'll have a real fight on your hands."

Sheila laughed heartily at that, then put up her hands defensively before pushing the cake across the table to Ernel. "I surrender, it's all yours."

Smiling, Ernel carefully cut the piece of cake in half and pushed half back to Sheila. "There will be no competition between us, my friend. We will share and share alike."

Matching her smile, Sheila retrieved the cake and took a small bite. "Oh, oh my oath, that is utterly divine. No wonder you were willing to put up a fight for it. What is this?"

"My mother's recipe, actually. It's made from the tea berries that Lilly Peters managed to resurrect. I talked to the chef about it, and he wanted to try. It took a few attempts, but he managed to get it right. I'm so glad you enjoyed it."

"You seem to have gone to a great deal of trouble for me, Ernel. Why?"

"Like me, you were alone and sad, mourning a loss of love. You befriended me, returned some of those good feelings to me. I wanted to do the same for you. Are you pleased?"

"Surprised, a bit bemused, and utterly delighted. Thank you."

"All my pleasure. Now, I can see the fatigue in your eyes, you need to rest. Off you go."

"Yes, dear," grinned Sheila. "Ernel?"

"Yes?"

"Breakfast before I head out tomorrow?"

"Love to. I'll be here." With a bright smile she waved and walked away.

Sheila watched her go then ran to Brandon's office where she requisitioned new quarters. As she lay back to rest that night, all she had with her was a fresh uniform for morning and her gift from Ernel. She plugged it into the system and drifted off to sleep to the sounds of birdsong.

Chapter #9

Elusive

While Sheila got her first good night's sleep in days, Ka'Ron sat waiting for his death to arrive. When he opened all the doors, he knew he'd given full access to the ship, both to the strangers and to the Wrax.

His memory wandered back over the past as he sat waiting, dozing in the captain's chair. Ka'Ron had been a young eager bridge officer when they'd been tossed across the galaxy to appear among dozens of crippled ships. The people of the different ships tried to work together, effect repairs, until the Wrax arrived.

The Wrax ship appeared and suddenly began spewing out hundreds of small fighters. Ship after ship exploded and began to spiral down to the planet below. A few, including his own fought back, but it was hopeless, the Wrax just kept killing and killing.

In desperation, two teams of infiltrators slipped into the huge Wrax ship to find it relatively empty. One team sought out the engine room and managed to complete their mission, the big ship would go no further.

The second team, Ka'Ron's team tried for the bridge, but were cut off. Alarms sounded from within the huge ship, doors slammed shut, and Ka'Ron's team was trapped.

It had taken them a while to understand what had happened. When the alarms sounded the Wrax stopped fighting and walked away. He had followed two of them to a small room where they set dials then climbed into cryo beds and pulled down the lids. All over the ship it was the same.

Even the small fighters outside stopped fighting and returned to the ship, a number didn't make it, shot down from behind. Ka'Ron had watched it all on the monitors from the bridge. He'd found only one man awake there, probably the captain, and shot him.

It had taken weeks to discover the ins and outs of the controls, but they'd managed, and eventually, when no help came, nor an answer to their calls for help, they'd given up and entered the cryo beds, Ka'Ron in the captain's.

Over the centuries the alarms had awakened him first every time. He would then shut off the alarms so the Wrax would not awaken, or so he hoped; it wasn't always successful. When he succeeded he'd call for help. No help had ever come, and eventually only his cryo bed was still functioning, he was the last of his team alive. Those ships that could escape did so, and the rest eventually crashed to the surface of the planet below.

Each time he would retreat to the cryo bed, but that would no longer help him, the bed was failing, and he dared not use it again. His only hope for survival depended on those new explorers, if only they would return ... and be quiet.

* * * * *

As Sheila entered her ship the crew was already there, looking at her. She was smiling and so were they. Ernel had met her for breakfast and insisted on hearing all about the exploration of the alien ship. After the meal, Ernel had walked her to the launch bay then stood watching as Sheila reached Retriever. She waved then turned away.

Facing all those smiling faces, Sheila was startled to feel color rise in her cheeks. "First one of you to say a word will be in a whole heap of trouble." There were several snickers as everyone turned their focus to their post. "Pilot, take us out."

"Aye, Captain, launching now."

"Return to the alien ship."

"Alien ship, aye." The agile scout ship was soon back where they had landed before.

Sheila sighed as she faced the crew. "Last time we were here we got some action, but our companion freaked out as well. We've got full sensors now so don't waste time exploring, just get to the bridge and see if you can locate our host."

Hal nodded as he fastened the helmet on his suit and stepped into the airlock. They were soon outside and following the voice of the comms operator as they got directions. It was a big ship, and a bit of a hike through partially familiar territory until they reached a bank of previously hidden elevators.

Using the translator, Hal found the button for the bridge and hit it. The machine rose smoothly for long moments then opened into another corridor. "Straight ahead and through the door," came the voice over the comms. Hal nodded then led off.

The door to the bridge was ajar, so he pushed it open. They all stepped in and began to cautiously poke around but saw nothing. "There's another door over here," said Twenty, as she pushed it aside and entered. It looked like the captain's quarters, including a cryo bed with the lid raised. It took a moment to locate the sound of the ragged breathing.

Twenty focused on another chair, and slowly a creature came into view holding a weapon. "We mean you no harm," she said, and the unit attached to her suit began to repeat the phrase in several different languages.

"You are the wild one, the one who makes noise and tries to kill us all."

Twenty tilted her head as she tried to make sense of what the translator said. "Lower your weapon, we won't harm you. We came to help."

"Help who, me or the Wrax?"

"I don't understand, who or what are the Wrax?"

"They are the destroyers of life, the death dealers sleeping on this ship. Your crashing around could set off the alarms to awaken them. I have never ..."

He got no further as Sessas intervened. She stepped in front of Twenty and gently pushed the creature's weapon aside. "No more talk. You weak, starving, tired, alone. Come." She took his weapon and tried to pull him to his feet, but he melted toward the floor. "Tentee carry. He too weak."

Twenty nodded and scooped the creature up in her arms. Hal radioed ahead that they had him and were on their way back. Sheila said the medical bay would be ready when they arrived. They were barely halfway to Retriever when a general alarm sounded throughout the ship and the big landing bay doors slammed shut.

"Retriever to Hal."

"Here, Captain. As I understand it, that alarm will wake up the sleeping giant. Our friend says we're all going to die."

"Maybe, but not today. Get a move on."

"Understood. All right, team, pick it up. Twenty, you need any help?"

"No, I've got him, just get going, I'll keep up."

They set out at a run, the others watching for any movement, and Sessas staying close to defend Twenty. They had to detour a couple of times but were all the way back to the cryo room before they encountered the Wrax. Barely half the cryo beds had responded to the alarm and no more than a dozen had live warriors inside.

It had been far too long for them all to have survived and the ship was damaged as well. Those who were awake just stared around stupidly, trying to get their bearings. "Keep going," gasped the alien in Twenty's arms. "They've got the cryo sickness, but it'll wear off soon."

"Run!" Hal led out at a run, but they had to pass through the room to get back to their ship.

One raised a weapon, but Sessas leaped ahead and brained him. She dropped two more before they started firing their weapons. "Assholes," she muttered, as she returned fire with her blaster.

Billy took a direct hit from a weapon that sent him flying, but the new armor protected him. He was still alive but injured. Rhonda hauled him to his feet, and they ran on. Suddenly a barrage of weapons fire drove the Wrax back. Sheila was there with the three extra security men that had been with them. Together they all made it back to Retriever and clambered inside.

"Assholes," grumbled Sessas, as she manned the ship's guns and opened fire.

"Sessas, the big doors," barked Sheila. Sessas swiveled the guns around and sent a missile into the launch bay doors. The doors buckled outwards, but not enough to let them escape. She fired another missile and this one had the desired effect. "Pilot, get us out. Comms, call the Reacher, we're coming home hot. Hal, report, what the hell happened?"

Several of the Wrax reached the small fighters and followed the Retriever out into open space. Retriever raced for the Reacher and safety, while more Wrax came pouring out of the crippled ship. As they neared Reacher the shields suddenly glowed red and Retriever was rocked.

* * * * *

Aboard Reacher, Jeannie was on the bridge as Sheila's call came in. "Get our shields up. Target that ship; fire as soon as Retriever is clear. A moment later Reacher was rocked by a blow from an unknown weapon, but the shields held. "Retriever is clear, Admiral."

"Fire!"

Reacher gave a gentle shudder and the huge alien ship was suddenly blown aside, half the hull buckling in. They watched the sensors as every Wrax fighter in free space turned as one and shot toward the wounded ship.

"Get all our people off the ground. Retriever, Friendship, EX2, battle stations. Protect our salvage ships." Retriever turned to watch the Wrax, the other two ships close behind him. They saw as both salvage vessels rose from the ground, headed for home as fast as they could go. The fleeing Wrax ignored them and vanished into the belly of the wounded war ship.

"Reacher, Retriever and sister ships escorting salvage ships home. We have injured aboard."

"Acknowledged, Retriever, come on home. Emmet, maintain alert status until further notice. Watch those sensors, you see movement, shoot first, ask questions later."

"Understood, Admiral."

Jeannie left the bridge and headed for the briefing room. The salvage ships were the first in, followed by Friendship, EX2, and then Retriever last. As the big landing bay doors closed the shields were reinforced. The crews were given only moments before the call came. "All captains and senior staff to the bridge."

Sheila was the last off her ship, as usual. Sessas and Twenty were escorting the medics as they hauled Ka'Ron off to the infirmary. "Hal, get a meal into everybody then put the ship back in order."

"Aye, Captain," he grinned in reply, as he headed for the mess hall.

A small figure caught Sheila's eye. Ernel was standing near the corridor, her eyes wide with concern. Sheila ran to her and took her gently by the shoulders. "Ernel, I'm all right. We had one injury, not me, and the alien needs attention, that's all. I'm fine."

Ernel smiled weakly and reached for Sheila's shoulders to give them a gentle squeeze. "That's a relief. I didn't want to lose my new best friend so soon."

Suddenly Sheila pulled her close and gave her a gentle hug. "Me either, girl. Listen, I'm fine, but half starved. Meet me in the mess after the meeting, I have lots of exciting things to tell you."

Ernel smiled and nodded as she stepped back from the hug. "Go on now, the admiral will be waiting." Sheila kissed her cheek then sped away.

* * * * *

"All senior staff and captains present, Admiral."

"Thank you, Brandon. Emmet, talk to me."

"Bridge is on full alert, shields at max, energy weapon charged, manned, and ready, Admiral."

"First Officer, status of the ship?"

"Ship is secure, Admiral. Our shields held and Reacher sustained no damage or injuries."

"That a relief. What's the status of the enemy ship?"

"The enemy sustained heavy damage and is now drifting freely in space."

"Good news indeed, thank you, Brandon. Captains?"

"EX2 is whole and sound, Admiral," replied Amanda.

"Friendship is good as new," smiled Linsey.

"Recovery One and Recovery Two are unharmed, Admiral," said Olga Volkov.

"Excellent. Medical?"

"No injuries for the Reacher, Admiral. Two only from satellite ships, the Retriever had one injured man and a starved alien. The injured man will be back on duty in a couple of days. I'd like to revive the alien a bit more before you interview him."

"Agreed, and thank you, Carla. All right now for it, Sheila, what the hell happened over there?"

"I guess we pushed our luck a bit too hard, Admiral. We got back inside without incident; all doors were open and there were no dead spots for comms and sensors. Hal and the team found the alien in the captain's quarters, nearly dead and hiding beside a non-functioning cryo bed. He was holding a weapon.

"Sessas stepped in, took the weapon then ordered SUVI 20 to carry him back to Retriever. They were halfway back when alarms started sounding all over the ship, the warriors began to revive, and the big bay doors slammed shut. Our people battled their way back, then we shot our way out and made a run for it.

"Billy took a hit from some sort of weapon, but the armor protected him. That's about it, Admiral, the rest you know."

"Well done, Sheila. Tell me, did we get anything useful from that ship besides the alien?"

"Rhonda and Sessas brought out a couple of weapons. Harlan is checking them out now, Linsey developed some sweet tech to help us, but all in all we didn't get a lot and we made enemies."

Jeannie sighed and sank back into her chair. "I see. Well, at the moment it appears the immediate threat has been neutralized. Moira, your thoughts?"

"There's still a few derelict ships I'd like to have a look at, see if we can get anything to improve our own tech, but that's all. The recovery ships had the last of the Earalith metals on board them, so we're good to go if you want to set sail."

Jeannie nodded. "Mandy, was there anything of interest on the second planet?"

"Just a few more dead ships and the leftovers of where the survivors had tried to colonize and failed," replied Captain Drake. "It was rich in plant life and Lilly filled her crates; she also got a bunch of samples from the first planet."

"Was the second planet likely?" asked Miriam Holbrooke, the passenger representative.

"Lilly says no, Miriam," replied Amanda. "She said it would rate a five or six at best. She wants at least an eight or better before she will recommend a planet."

Several people chuckled at that. "Ah yes," said Miriam, "the Lilly Peters scale of planetary evaluation. Well I, for one, trust her judgement. Commander Peters says no, then it's no."

"So, shall I prepare to set sail, Admiral?"

"Not just yet, Emmet, however, move us away from this immediate area and over closer to the second planet. That way, if those fighter ships come after us, we'll have more warning. Right now, I want a word with our new guest before we leave this system.

"Sheila, your assessment of your ship and crew under fire."

"Friendship Two is a marvel, Admiral, and he performed above expectation. The same for my crew. These people were careful, yet cool under fire. Sessas and Twenty are a couple of free thinkers, yet they performed well as part of a team. I'm quite pleased with my crew, Admiral."

"Excellent. Moira, how's her new ship coming along?"

"Almost ready for test flights, Admiral. She'll be a bit bigger than Friendship 2, tougher with better weapons and shields, however, the crew will have to work a bit harder as we don't have an AI core for her, and Dorind has no idea how to make one."

"Hal will be happy to hear that, Moira," grinned Sheila. "He says he hasn't been able to stand up straight for days. Personally, I find Friendship 2 quite comfortable and good company."

That brought a round of chuckles. "You'll have to take along someone else to talk to," grinned Jeannie. "I believe I may have seen you talking to a possible candidate as you left the ship."

Sheila blushed and shook a finger at Amanda. "Amanda Drake, I'm embarrassed and it's all your fault. I curse the day you taught Admiral Sorenson how to tease a human."

"On that note, people, get some rest," chuckled Jeannie. "Emmet, move us over to the other planet but keep us on high alert."

The meeting broke up and Sheila headed for the mess. She found Ernel waiting with two plates of food. "What, real food, no desserts?" she asked, as she sat down facing Ernel.

"I realized I need to be paying better attention to your nutrition," was the grinning reply.

"Yes, Mom," chuckled Sheila, as she tucked in with a will.

"So, tell me all the exciting news."

Smiling, Sheila related her adventures while she ate her meal. "The admiral saw you waiting for me and suggested I take you with me on the new ship, so I'll have someone to talk to instead of an AI."

Ernel chuckled at that. "Oh no, you're the adventurous one, not me. You go play then come back to me with tales of high adventure."

"You don't even want to go out for a look?"

"Sure, if you find something beautiful to show me, but you say there's nothing here but broken ships."

Sheila reached over to take her by the hands. "Ernel, I'm sorry for that. I didn't mean to remind you of ..."

"Hush now," said Ernel, as she squeezed the hands that held her, "hush, it's all right. I know you didn't. Just find me something beautiful and inspiring, and then I'll gladly go for a ride in your new ship."

"I will, I promise I will at first opportunity."

Ernel gave her hands another gentle squeeze then stood. "Stay there, I'll be right back with dessert."

"Dessert? I get dessert too?"

"Indeed you do. Chef made another cake; this time I'm getting us a bigger piece to share." Sheila smiled with delight as she watched the tiny woman walk away.

* * * * *

While Sheila enjoyed her meal and the company, Jake returned to his office where Hal and Rhonda were waiting for him. "Hi guys, waiting long?"

"Not long," replied Hal, as he eased himself out of Jake's chair. "What's up, big brother?"

"You know damn well what's up, Hal. I'm the new guy on this chief of security job, our dream job. Commander Hoffman is mentoring me as best he can, but he's a busy man. The rest of the crew know I'm a newbie and a few of them have tested me a bit."

"You dealt with that, I expect," grinned Hal.

"Yeah, just like Dad taught us, hard and fast, but there's a bit of resentment floating around right now. That's why I called you two in here. I need a second-in-command, somebody to play good cop to my bad. George is covering for now, but he's retiring next week so the job is open. It's yours if you want it, Hal."

Hal sighed and settled back into a chair. "I know, Jake, and up until a week ago I'd have jumped at it."

"But?"

"Things have changed. With you as chief of security, your number two is as far as I could go, ever. Don't get me wrong, you and I make an awesome team, we've proved that over and over since you came to work in security."

"But?"

"But with my new job, I can learn a ton from Captain Singh, and when she's ready to retire in a few years, I'll be next in line to captain the Retriever, maybe get a ship of my own sooner if we build more. Jake, I'll always work with you when we're on the Reacher, you know that, but ..."

"Yeah, Twenty told me you'd say that. Go for it, Hal. Be careful, learn what you can, and ..."

"And watch Twenty's back? Jake, you know I will. So, you're okay with me staying on Retriever? I know we always planned to be the dream team on Security."

"Yeah, I'm good here, little brother, go ahead, show me up, make captain, just keep my wife in one piece."

"I'll guard her with my life, Jake, I promise."

Jake nodded then turned his attention to Rhonda. "Ensign Rhonda Moore."

"Yes, Commander Jake White?"

She was grinning and he chuckled as he spun the monitor on his desk around where she could see it. "This is your service record, impressive to say the least. Rhonda, we've worked together on a few issues and you impressed me, this record impresses me. Of all the security people available to me, you just went to the top of the list when Hal turned down the job.

"Look, I know there are a lot of more senior people, but Admiral Sorenson believes in promoting people by proven ability, not by seniority. By her standards, which I endorse completely, you're the strongest candidate for the job. Your record is a match for Hal's or mine and you know it. The job's yours if you want it."

Rhonda was silent for a few moments, then Hal spoke. "Take it, Rhonda. You deserve it, you know that."

She nodded. "Yeah, I can't deny I had ambitions. It was always between you and me, Hal, before Jake came along. You and I work well together, but we were always jostling for the same promotions. All right, Commander White, I accept the post. When do I start?"

"Tomorrow. Rhonda, it'll take you a while to get your legs under you with this. George has said he'll stay another week or so to help you settle in. Your new rank will be Sub-Commander. Go requisition new uniforms. Oh, and it's okay to go out with Retriever for a while until Hal gets another recruit settled in.

"Now, Hal, I know damn well you're going to plunder my department for Rhonda's replacement. Who are you going to steal?"

Hal gave a soft chuckle. "I don't know, I'll have to see the lists."

"You don't work for me anymore; Rhonda, don't let him near the lists."

"Whoa, play nice, boys, besides, I don't start my new job until tomorrow. Not getting in the middle here, guys."

Jake just grinned. "You're a wise woman, Sub-Commander Moore. Hal, I know Rayla Mills has been training with you guys. Woman's tough as nails and bored to tears."

"Yeah, Rayla would be my first choice. I'll go talk to her."

"And I'll go get a new uniform and be back here first thing tomorrow." Rhonda was smiling brightly as she fairly danced out of Jake's office to hurry back to quarters. She was wearing her new uniform when she arrived at the mess. Still grinning, she feigned wide-eyed innocence as Sheila Singh shook a finger at her.

Rhonda was still enjoying her meal as Sheila and Ernel rose to leave. Sheila smiled and patted Rhonda on the shoulder as she walked by. "Congratulations, Sub-Commander, I believe Jake made a wise choice."

"Thank you, Captain, it means a lot to me that you approve." Sheila patted her shoulder again then reached for Ernel's hand as they walked away.

Chapter #10

Ka'Ron

"What is it, Jeannie? What's bugging my super SUVI?" asked Amanda, as she approached and sat beside Jeannie in their cuddling chair.

Jeannie sighed and laid her head on Amanda's shoulders. "Mandy, I'm terribly afraid."

"Of what, my love?"

"I'm afraid that I've lost my SUVI self and become human."

Amanda gazed at her for a moment then kissed her forehead. "Explain."

"Mandy, any good SUVI would have moved the Reacher away from that ship the moment it turned toward us. No SUVI in her right mind would have sent a ship onto it, nor would she have let them stay the instant she knew it was a war ship. Moreover, she would never have sent them back after a single survivor, risking the entire crew of that ship to rescue a dying stranger.

"No, instead I indulged Twenty and Sheila like a doting human grandmother, sent them where they had no business being, risked their lives, and all for what? What did we gain? What benefit to the greater good was accomplished? We gained no resources and made dangerous enemies in the process."

Amanda sighed and hugged Jeannie tightly. "I understand, sweet Suvi-jean, I do. Can I ask why you did that, I mean, why did you send them out in the first place?"

"It was Twenty's excitement, she wanted to check it out so badly and I, too, sensed something important was over there."

"So, you're saying you used your SUVI intuition plus trusted the instincts of a fellow SUVI to guide your decision, is that right?"

"Yes."

"Okay, why didn't you recall them when they reported all the small fighter ships and sleeping warriors?"

"I couldn't, not without destroying their confidence. They've been training to go into dangerous situations to retrieve our people should the need arise. Pulling them back would tell them I didn't trust their judgement."

"But you let them go back to save the alien, why?"

"Because they wanted to, it's what they were trained to do, it was a chance to let them show their mettle, to prove to themselves and everybody that they're ready."

"Okay, now let me give you a different perspective. First you trusted your own SUVI instincts and Twenty's as well, a truly SUVI thing to do. Second, you trusted them to perform their tasks for the greater good, which they did. They explored the war ship, made several discoveries, encountered issues that forced Linsey to invent new and better tools, and overcame those difficulties.

"Furthermore, you sent them to rescue the alien, to test themselves, trusting in their abilities to perform their tasks as needed. When they came running out with the fugitive, you destroyed the enemy ship that was attacking your people, removing the threat to the greater population."

"Yes, but I should have just moved us away when it was apparent the ship wasn't completely dead."

"Dear, sweet, Suvi-jean, your instincts are to serve the greater good, but we're a lost and abandoned people, we have no home but Reacher, and to sustain ourselves we must glean whatever resources we can. We can't always take the safest road, even a SUVI knows that.

"Jeannie, if all your people were SUVI you could act one way, but most of us are human, and there are the Earalith as well. You're forced to consider us all and take all our needs into account when you make your decisions. This forces you to do things differently.

"An example is the planet where we encountered the energy beam. Because of that we now have strong defensive weapons on the Reacher. Who knows what will come of this adventure? Sweetheart, not always taking the safest road doesn't make you less of a SUVI, it makes you a better leader."

"Yeah?"

"Yeah."

"You truly believe that?"

"I do."

"You don't think I'm becoming too human?"

"No love," chuckled Amanda, "but I do have a suggestion."

"Oh?"

"Yes, before starting each day, take the time to meditate and bring the SUVI warrior up to the surface."

"You mean the huntress."

"No, love, I mean the warrior. We have other SUVI hunters to sustain us. We need a warrior to lead and defend us."

Jeannie squirmed around in the chair to gaze into Amanda's eyes. "Mandy, are you certain about this?"

"Yes, I'm sure. Jeannie, I can always tell when you've been suppressing your true nature for the comfort of the herd, us humans. Honey, we're a desperate people, trying to come back from the brink. We need you at full power."

"All right, Mandy, if you're sure. I'll start first thing in the morning."

With a soft purring growl Amanda grabbed Jeannie by the shoulders and pulled her close. "No, right now, Suvi-jean. Do it now."

Jeannie's eyes turned amber as she rose to her feet, seized Amanda and tossed her over her shoulder. Amanda shrieked as she was dropped on the bed and pounced upon by her warrior SUVI. "Oh yeah, that's my SUVI woman."

* * * * *

It was early the next day when Linsey brought Ka'Ron to the admiral's briefing room and introduced him to the senior staff and captains. "Welcome, Ka'Ron," said the Admiral. "You have learned our language?"

"I have, great Admiral, and I thank you for ordering my rescue. I had long since given up hope."

"You weren't native to that warship?"

"No, I was a saboteur, the only survivor of two separate parties sent to destroy it. We managed to cripple it, but no more."

"Start at the beginning, tell us how you came to be in control of the ship."

"Yes, ma'am. Our ship, and its sister ship were locked together for an exchange of resources when they were seized by some force and hurled here halfway across the galaxy. We suffered damage and, with the help of a few others ships and species, were making repairs.

"That's when the Wrax arrived. Without a single moment's hesitation, they attacked, destroying several wounded ships before we could mount any kind of defense. Our sister ship fled into hyperspace, but I have no idea if they survived, for she was badly damaged and should not have attempted the jump.

"We were fighting a desperate battle but saw our chance. With her launch bay doors open to spew out the small fighters, the Wrax ship was vulnerable. Two teams transported aboard. Team one managed to destroy their engines but perished in the task.

"When the engines blew, a strange thing happened. The Wrax stopped fighting, the small ships returned to the mother, and the pilots put themselves into cryo sleep. On the upper levels, I also saw the resistance fade away as the crew put themselves into cryo sleep as well. The ship's defenses went up to full alert and no efforts could break through.

"My team found the bridge and disabled the distress signals being sent out. Only then did I learn our own ship had been destroyed utterly. Until the alarms sounded, we were in a heated battle. When the fighting stopped, we followed them and took over their cryo beds, eventually I was the only one to survive.

"We found and disabled the cryo beds of the bridge crew, killing them all. I then recorded a distress message of my own and sent it out on auto, to broadcast whenever a new ship might appear.

"For months we prowled that accursed ship until only I was left, seeking an escape, but there was none to be found.

"The Wrax are of two separate species, the rulers, and the slave fighters. Their ships are built so that they cannot intermingle.

"It is only by hidden passageway can one access different parts of the ship. My problem was keeping the fighters asleep until someone found me, or I could find a way out. Many failed before your people succeeded.

"When I fully realized the situation I was in, I began to study the Wrax and their ship. I soon learned that they're completely evil, living only for the glory of the kill. As I was studying them, another ship was brought here through the portal. Alarms awakened the Wrax.

"I hid while the captain emerged from his quarters, released the fighters who attacked and destroyed the new ship, then went back into cryo, waiting for repair ships to arrive. When this happened a second time, I killed that captain while he was in the frozen sleep then took his place in the bed.

"From time to time the alarms would awaken me, and to my horror I would watch helplessly as another ship was destroyed. The fighters then swept over the planet to make sure nothing lived, and then they returned to their beds.

"Each time the same, awaken, kill, destroy, then return to sleep awaiting rescue and repairs. Eons have passed I'm sure, and the beds are failing, no longer able to sustain the sleeping forms."

"Including you," said Jeannie.

"Yes, you were my last hope, but eventually, even as your people reached me, the alarms finally triggered the beds and the Wrax awakened. Fortunately, none were alive on the bridge to bring the ship's main weapons into play. Your ship could not have survived that."

"Fortunate indeed. Now we're at a point where we must decide on our next move."

"What are you going to do with me?"

"You say that eons have passed, and the only survivors of your people left long ago. For now, I'd like to keep you with us, avail ourselves of your knowledge, etc. Should we ever encounter more of your species you will be free to join them or remain with us. Is this acceptable to you?"

"It is, Admiral. Am I to be held slave or prisoner?"

"We keep no slaves on this ship, my friend, nor will you be held prisoner. Hopefully you will find a way to fit in, make yourself useful, find friends, build a life here among the many. Most of us are human, a few are SUVI, some are Earalith, and we have one Saurian." Jeannie grinned at him. "You'll add even more to the mix. Tell me, Ka'Ron, what are your people called?"

"We are ... I am a Morar."

"You are welcome here, friend Ka'Ron of the Morar. You have endured much and survived; I admire that. Tell me, have you met Antha yet?"

"Yes, Sessas dragged her to my bedside as soon as I awakened."

"It seems our Sessas has adopted you. I'll call her to get you set up." Jeannie reached for her comm. "Sorenson to Sessas."

"Sessas."

"Sessas, come to the briefing room and get Ka'Ron, set him up with quarters then take him to the mess and feed him."

"Coming."

Jeannie chuckled at that as she let her arm fall away from the comm. "She's a woman of few words, our Sessas." A moment later there was a soft tap at the door, Sessas entered, took Ka'Ron by the arm and led him away.

As they left Jeannie arose and began pacing around the room. "All right people, opinions?"

"I believe his story, Admiral," said Sheila. "What he said jives with what we know and saw aboard that ship. SUVI 20 nearly lost her lunch when they found that trophy room. We know every ship in the area has been cut apart and destroyed."

"I agree with Sheila," said Jake. "Still, I want to keep an eye on him for a while, you know, just in case."

"Do it, Jake. All right, are we finished here, are we ready to set sail?"

"Ship is secure and ready for travel, Admiral."

"Thank you, Brandon. Emmet?"

"Bridge is ready when you are, Admiral."

"Captains, are your ships secure inside Reacher?"

"All ships aboard and secure, Admiral," smiled Amanda.

"Moira, have you any reason to hang around?"

"Nothing really, just a bit of curiosity, Jeannie. Engineering is good to go."

"All right then, Captain da Silva."

"Admiral?"

"Set up a beacon with as many languages as you have, warning incoming ships of the Wrax on that damaged ship. This and no more can we do for those who follow us through the rift.

"Emmet, aim us at the next system and, as soon as Linsey launches her beacon, we'll set sail."

"At once, Admiral. Shall I maintain alert status until we sail?"

"Absolutely."

* * * * *

Ka"Ron sat in his new quarters, smiling. This was so much more than he'd hoped for, survival as a prisoner was the best he had imagined. Across from him sat the Saurian female who'd kept him alive, for as he sank to the floor facing the aliens he'd tried to enlist, he'd seen his death in the big warrior's eyes.

The fingers of his hand had refused to respond to the command to release the weapon. Before the big one could fire, the Saurian had taken command, stripped away the weapon, then ordered another to carry him. Ka'Ron owed her his life, but he wondered why she'd done it. He wanted to ask, but that unblinking gaze of her's made him nervous.

Finally he roused his courage and spoke. "Thank you for these wonderful quarters, are your own close?"

"Yesss," she nodded, the translation device she wore struggling to make her speech intelligible.

"You saved my life, and I'm deeply grateful."

"Yesss?"

"May I ask why?"

She took a few moments before she responded. "Not asshole, afraid, weak, hungry, alone."

"So, I aroused your maternal instincts, did I?"

She thought for a moment the waggled her hand in the air. "Maybe. Mission was to find you, help if possible. We find, help. Now your turn."

"My turn? I don't understand, my turn for what?"

"Help us."

"I would be thrilled to help you, to repay in some small measure the kindness shown me. How? How can I help your people?"

"Ask SUVI 5, she leader, she tell."

"SUVI 5, you mean the admiral?"

"Yesss."

"But they interviewed me, she said nothing ..."

"When she ready."

"I see. I will confess to you; she frightens me more than the Wrax."

The hissing sound that came from her throat must have been laughter. "Yesss, scary SUVI 5, but strong, good leader, protect all people. SUVI protect all people, SUVI 5 protect SUVI too. You rest now. I come back later."

She rose and started to the door. "Sessas?" She turned back to gaze at him, her head tilted slightly to the side. "I have seen you perform a certain ritual with several people where you hug them, and they kiss the top of your head. What does that mean?"

"It means they friends, family."

"You did this with the admiral, is she your friend too?"

"SUVI 5 good friend to Sessas, like Sessas, keep, save life. Ka'Ron work hard, help people, earn place, be friend, family. Rest now."

With that she was gone, and he was alone again, but not as before. A live ship filled with living people surrounded him, a friend had spent time with him, he'd eaten actual food, and now he could rest.

Ka'Ron crawled onto the bed and sighed deeply as he fairly melted into it, a real bed, not a metal and glass tube with sharp needles to jab into him to make him sleep. This time he was warm and safe. He brushed the fur back from his eyes then closed them as he drifted off, a smile on his lips for the first time in centuries.

Sessas turned the corner to her own quarters to find Jeannie and Twenty waiting for her. They hugged her and kissed the top of her head and she squeaked with delight then opened the door and let them in, indicating they should sit. "Sessas happy see friends. Why come?"

"Can't fool you, can I Sessas," grinned Jeannie.

"SUVI 5 busy always."

"Yes I am, my friend, and I admit I have a reason for the visit. Sessas, do you trust Ka'Ron?"

Sessas waggled her hand in the air and Twenty laughed. "Sessas get it right, Tentee?"

"You got it right, honey. Yes, he's still an unknown. We have no reason to mistrust him, but there was that weapon when we found him."

"Tell me about that, Twenty."

"When we found him he was hiding, sort of, and holding a weapon. Hal was about to fire when Sessas took over."

"Sessas, why did you step in?"

"Ka'Ron weak, eyes watery, fearful, shaky, weapon not working. He know much, not tell when dead."

Jeannie nodded her approval. "My dear Sessas, there is more to you than we realize. That was well done. He now knows you as his savior, his protector. He'll trust you, both of you. Keep an eye on him for me?"

"Yesss. He say he want to help SUVI 5, help people. You ask, he say what he know."

"And I'll do just that," smiled Jeannie, as she rose and hugged Sessas again. "Thank you, Sessas. You've become valuable to us all and we're delighted you chose to come with us."

Sessas fairly purred as she returned the hug. "Sessas happy too." Twenty joined the hug then left with Jeannie. Sessas curled up in a ball on the bed and went to sleep, smiling.

* * * * *

While Jeannie and Twenty took their leave of Sessas, there was another parting. Sheila had held Ernel's hand all the way back to the small woman's quarters. When they reached to door, Ernel invited her in and showed off her larger quarters, family quarters, but Commander Hoffman had given them to her so she could set up a studio.

Sheila marveled at some of the works in progress, Ernel did love bright colors, but then, so did Sheila. As she took her leave she impulsively hugged the smaller woman and lightly kissed her on the head. "I'll bet Sessas taught you that," came the soft chuckle from her shoulder as Ernel returned the hug.

Sheila laughed heartily, her first real laugh in a long time and she reveled in it. "She did not," she denied, "but it's a good idea."

"Yes it is, now hug me again, for it's been eons since I've been hugged by someone who likes me."

"Well then, I'll have to hug you often, you've got a lot of catching up to do. Good night, dear friend."

"Good night, sweet Sheila. Meet me for breakfast?"

"I'll come for you, wait for me?"

"I will." Smiling, Ernel lightly kissed her cheek and withdrew into the apartment. Sheila had a renewed spring in her step as she returned to her own quarters.

Chapter #11

Moving On

Sheila didn't get her breakfast. She was just leaving her quarters when the call came over the comms. "Battle stations, battle stations, all captains to your ships, Admiral to the bridge."

Jeannie arrived at the bridge even as Commander Jones reached for the comms and Anita gave the warning from her sensor station. "What?"

"Incoming fighter ships."

"Where? How many?"

"Could be a hundred or more, Admiral, coming from the Wrax ship."

"Shields. Emmet, are we locked down?"

"Locked down, all ships are aboard, the beacon has been launched, star drive is fully charged and a course to the next system is laid in."

"Hit it." At her command the Reacher shuddered slightly then vanished from the danger zone and hurtled toward the nearest star system.

"Ship is away, Admiral."

"Are we being followed?"

"No. Those are fighter ships, Admiral, designed to fight in space or an atmosphere. They wouldn't have room for a star drive, nor would they need one. The warship would carry them wherever they needed to go."

"Yes, of course. Best guess at travel time?"

"The next system is fairly close. With our new engines I'd say two weeks, no more."

"Well done, Emmet. Stand down alert, call the captains and senior staff to the briefing room."

* * * * *

"All requested personnel present, Admiral."

"Thank you, Brandon. Relax people, we're clear. I had a sense something was wrong, of danger. I was heading for the bridge when the call came. It seems that, when we demonstrated the power of our weapon, the Wrax went back to wake up as many of the others as they could. I'd say they came at us with everything they had.

"However, our bridge crew was fully prepared, and we got away clean. Their warship is crippled so they can't follow us. Now, tell me we have no reason to go back there."

"We have no reason at all to go back there," grinned the first officer.

Jeannie chuckled at that, allowing her eyes to return to their natural green. "Good, now, what did we get out of that system, anything and everything that might be useful. Moira?"

"From an engineering standpoint, we did quite well, Jeannie. Amanda managed to find an Earalith battle cruiser to salvage. We finished all repairs to Reacher, topped up our metals, improved our weapons, and Frank's got an Earalith war cruiser engine in his cargo hold. Dorind says it'll never work again, but by taking it apart we can learn a bunch of good things, greatly improve our speed, and make use of the metals."

"How's our supply of good metal?"

"We're good. I think it's safe to put EX4 back on the list of possibles."

"Good to know. Brandon?"

"Well, Admiral, we also gained useful tech, not so much alien tech, but tech created by Captain da Silva in response to an immediate need. We field tested our new Retriever class ship and crew as well as adding a lot of knowledge."

"Such as?"

"We learned that the galaxy is, or was at one time, teaming with life in a myriad of forms, some friendly, some not. Sheila's crew brought information about dozens of races."

"From the trophy collection of the Wrax, yes?"

"Yes."

"And you say the galaxy was teeming with life, but not so much now because everything we've encountered so far has been ancient ruins, the remains of ancient races, old derelict ships, etc."

"Yes. I'm starting to get the sense that humans and SUVI may be the youngest species so far. Perhaps that's why Earth was thought to be the sole supporter of intelligent life, everything else had passed into the mystery of time before humanity was born."

"An interesting theory, but I won't count on it. We also learned something else there, we're vulnerable if we encounter a truly aggressive race. We're a lone ship, a ship that was designed to carry passengers in comfort, not to fight or survive a battle.

"Engineering, can you put energy shields and better weapons on all our small ships?"

"Friendships One and Two are already equipped with the best weapons we can muster. We can add energy shields, no problem. EX2 and Retriever are already armed, and the extra shields are easy enough."

"Do it, Moria. Jake."

"Yes?"

"Twenty and Sessas brought back some small arms, has Harlan had a chance to check them out?"

"He says one of them is way better than anything we've got now. He's working on producing a few for security."

"Get him some help, I want those new weapons available to all small ship crews as well as security."

"I'll get right on it, Admiral."

"Carla, what news?"

"We're all good in medical. Most of the injuries incurred when we got tossed over here have healed."

"Most?"

"A few will never heal fully, and a number of others need more time."

"Understood."

"I do have a bit of good news, Jeannie."

"Hit me with it, Carla, I need good news."

"We have a total of two hundred and seven pregnant women aboard the Reacher."

Jeannie's eyes lit up with delight. "We do? Oh, that is good news. What brought this on?"

"A lot of bored passengers I expect, plus the embryos Dr. Reilly revived."

"Eamon?"

"Ah Jeannie, among the useful things confiscated from those men sent into exile was another crate of viable embryos. Since you'd told me to get all possible embryos into the gene pool, I call for volunteers. Actually, most of them came from our own crew. It seems the passengers prefer to do it the old-fashioned way."

"I'm glad to hear that," smiled Jeannie. "Well, it now seems we have a bit of time to reflect. We'll meet again in two days' time to take another look at the situation. Get some rest, people."

As the meeting broke up Sheila hurried to the mess. She found Ernel sitting alone at a table, working on something in her hand. "You waited for me?"

"I did. Sit now and I'll bring you food."

"You sit and I'll get the food." She was away before Ernel had a chance to protest. A few moments later Sheila was back with their breakfasts.

"I could have gotten that for you."

"Ernel, believe me when I say I love the way you nurture me, but you were working, and I interrupted you, caused a distraction."

Smiling, Ernel laid her work aside and addressed her breakfast. "Perhaps, but a pleasant distraction. So, since you're here smiling at me, I can assume the battle is over, yes?"

"It didn't happen. They came at us in force, but the ship was already on full alert. The admiral gave the order and we vanished from that system. The Wrax were too slow, and we got away clean."

"I like the way the admiral thinks, it is most reassuring."

"Oh?"

"An Imperial ship would never have avoided the battle. However, Reacher isn't a war ship, she's a home for thousands of people, only a few of them warriors. She protects the people above all else. I like that."

"Yes, and so do I. Now, what are you working on there?"

"This? Oh, it's a surprise for someone special."

"Really? Anyone I know?"

"Possibly." Ernel's sly grin gave it away, and as Sheila arched an eyebrow at her she began to giggle. "Oh all right, I'll show it to you."

She pushed the working tablet across the table to Sheila. It was a partially finished picture of an old Earth sailing vessel under full sail. "It's amazing."

"Look closer." Sheila took another look and then she saw it. Enlarging the section where the captain stood at the wheel, she saw her own face. "An ancestor of someone I know perhaps?"

Sheila laughed at that. "Ernel, you're amazing, the detail here, hey, are those extra wrinkles on my face there?"

"They are not, for you have no such thing on your face."

"Sadly girl, I really do."

"Only those caused by laughter, and they don't count."

"Thank you for that. Now, I fear I must get to my ship. Want to come along and let me show you around?"

"I'm aware that others have noticed me waiting for your ship when it returns. This won't cause you to endure further teasing, will it?"

"Not if they know what's good for them. Come on, let me show you my toys. We're interstellar right now, nothing really to do on the ship."

* * * * *

While Ernel got a tour of Retriever, Ka'Ron sat nervously facing the admiral, Captain Drake, and First Officer. Finally he caved to the tension and spoke. "Have I committed some offense?"

"Not at all," replied Jeannie, "I just want to discuss a few things with you."

"Of course, Admiral."

"You said that, when the Wrax attacked, one of your ships escaped."

"Yes, but she was badly damaged, I have no idea if she managed to survive or not."

"If she survived, where would she go?"

"They would have tried for the nearest star system; they wouldn't have a hope of reaching any other."

"And that's where we're bound," said Jeannie. "Brandon?" He just nodded so Jeannie turned to Amanda. "Mandy, all yours."

Amanda Drake smiled as she addressed Ka'Ron. "When we arrive at the next system, I'd like you to join my crew."

"Oh, why me?"

"Those were your people; you'll know what to look for. There may even be some of their descendants there, or perhaps some sign that they made repairs and went on. If there are people there you may be able to talk to them. That would be a big help to us in that case. What do you say, will you sign on?"

"Yes, of course. I'd be honored, Captain Drake."

"Thank you. I'll ask Linsey to work with you so she can have a translation device ready for us when we make planetfall."

Ka'Ron chuckled. "She's already working on it. That's where I was when you called for me."

"Perfect. First thing tomorrow, join me at EX2 and I'll show you around, help familiarize you with the ship and her functions. All crew members are familiar with every station, but each has a specialty. Welcome aboard."

He thanked her then left to find Sessas waiting for him just outside the door. "All is well?"

"Yes, Mother Sessas, all is well. I've been asked to join the crew of EX2, the explorer ship."

"Is good ship, good crew. Watch out for Thirteen, he gets cranky."

"Sessas, my dear friend, I hate it that I can never tell when you're teasing."

"Good," she replied, but her hissing laughter gave the game away.

He rolled his eyes as he hurried along behind her. Her species were obviously more adapted for speed than his, and he struggled to keep up with her. Ka'Ron sighed with relief as he saw she'd led him to the mess hall for a meal. At least she'd let him sit while they ate.

* * * * *

While Ernel got her tour and Ka'Ron got breakfast, Jake and Rhonda were in his office. Jake grinned as he spoke. "See, I knew you were a keener. You've been on the job, what, an hour? Already you're in here with an issue I didn't know about."

"Oh bull, you know. EX2 needs a new security guy since Hal took the job with Retriever."

"Yeah, I knew. Recovery needs a new security officer too."

"Oh?"

"Marcus took early retirement."

"So that's what happened."

"Excuse me?"

"Captain Singh, she had the blues for a while, then we noticed her holding hands with an Earalithian woman. She and Marcus must have split up."

"No doubt, probably for the best."

"Oh?"

"Captain Singh is small and gorgeous, but she's deadly at hand to hand combat. Marcus kept insisting he train with her."

"He got his ass kicked repeatedly and didn't like it?" asked Rhonda.

"That's my guess," said Jake.

"Men."

"Hey."

"Oops."

"You're damned right, oops. Just for that you get to assign the new security to the small ships."

She chuckled at that. "Any suggestions?"

"Rhonda, I want young, eager, fast, and smart people on those ships. I know there were a few disappointed people when Hal chose the crew for Retriever. Are there any likely prospects there?"

"Connie Kim is smart and lightning fast, plus a genius with all kinds of weapons. I'd put her on EX2."

"Sounds perfect, Rhonda, and you and I both know she has a thing for Thirteen. So, what about for Recovery?"

"I like Dave Gruber for the job. Dave's good, but a bit older and as much of a tinkerer as a security guy. I think he's a good fit for Recovery."

"Yeah, I think Dave would love Harlan's job, but Recovery sounds like the right place for him for now. Okay, I'll go talk to the captains then let you know."

Rhonda returned to her new desk and Jake sought out Amanda. They spoke for a while and Amanda agreed with his choice. Jake then found Captain Volkov. She agreed with his choice too, so he called Rhonda as he walked away. "Jake to Sub-Commander Moore."

"Rhonda here."

"It's a go. Call Connie and Dave in for their new assignments."

"Understood."

* * * * *

So it began, for days the newly assigned people settled into their new jobs. Ka'Ron was still resting up as best he could, but Captain Drake kept him busy learning what he could of EX2. He was impressed, both with the tough little ship and her captain. SUVI 13 frightened him.

Chapter #12

Arrival

Suvi-jean was on the bridge as the Reacher dropped down to sub-light speed. They were in a single star system. "All stop."

"All stop, aye. Ship has stopped, Admiral."

"Thank you, Emmet. Anita, what's the good word?"

"Standard single star system, Admiral, seventeen planets in all, only one in the Goldilocks zone."

"See anything in the air?"

"Nothing moving, Admiral, no artificial satellites we can detect, and no debris that would indicate it had once been a work of technology."

"All right then, take us in closer, Emmet. Head for the likely one in the Zone, then we'll let Amanda loose with her new ship."

The second officer nodded to the pilot, who adjusted his controls, and the mighty Reacher began to move forward. "We'll be in orbit by start of shift tomorrow, Admiral."

"Thank you, Emmet. Call a full staff meeting, I'll be in the briefing room."

* * * * *

"All senior staff, ships captains, and passenger representatives present, Admiral."

"Thank you, Brandon. All right, people, we're nearly there. Start of shift tomorrow we'll be in orbit. Brandon, what are we short on, what do we need most for Reacher?"

"For starters I'd like to open up all the extra hydroponics bays."

"Seriously? We're not even at half capacity for population, what's the big need there?"

"Two things, Jeannie. First, since Lilly Peters was able to get some Earalithian Tea Berries into production there's been a sudden surge of demand for the tea."

"I know," smiled Jeannie. "I fear I'm one of the offenders. What's the second thing?"

"Metals," replied Brandon. "Moira?"

"We're good for Earalithian metals, Jeannie, but what we've got is the last of it. I have the means to make more, but it'll take time. I'd also like to see if we can find some of the rarer metals we need.

"What I'd like to do is learn if the system has what we need, and then set up a smelter to see if we can produce our own, how long that would take, etc. My hope is we can talk a few of the passengers into becoming metalsmiths. Dorind says he can teach us how to set up a small operation."

"Okay, anything else we need to top up on?"

"Not that I'm aware of, Admiral," said Brandon Hoffman. "However, if that planet looks good for possible sources for different foods it might be nice."

Jeannie nodded thoughtfully. "All right, Amanda, EX2 gets the planet in the goldilocks Zone. Captain Volkov, you start poking around some of the other planets, see what you can find. Maybe take Dorind with you.

"Linsey, have you got that translation device for Ka'Ron's language ready yet?"

"Three made up and Captain Drake has them on her ship, Admiral."

"Then we're good to go. Amanda, be careful, take no chances. If EX2 gives the all-clear for the planet, we can send out Recovery One, Friendship, and Retriever to investigate some of the other others.

"Brandon, start recruiting for possible miners and metalsmiths. Maybe if Moira can get EX4 into service it can become a mining scout or something like that."

"I'll look into it, Admiral."

"Medical, how are things in your department?"

"We're good," smiled Carla. "We could use a few more sources of certain medicines; Dr. Reilly has given Lilly a list of what we could make use of. She said she'd test everything she can find to see if she can top us up."

"Excellent, then we're as ready as we can be. As soon as we reach orbit Captain Singh will take her ship and run a fast scout through the system to make sure there are no surprises hiding anywhere. Once she gives the go ahead then EX2 can investigate the planet.

"We have a plan, folks. Get some rest, tomorrow will be a busy day."

* * * * *

"So, what's all the excitement?" asked Ernel, as she and Sheila hurried along to the mess for breakfast.

"Excitement?"

"I can feel the tension in you, you're itching to tell me something."

"Busted. Okay, today I get to take you for that ride on my ship. We're in a new system, no signs of advanced technology anywhere, just the natural beauty of a star system. Please, Ernel, say you'll come."

"I'd love to. I've never actually seen anything like that before. Yes, I've travelled through space on ships, but never saw more than the inside of the ship.

"Here, you sit while I fetch the food."

"You always get the trays; shouldn't I take a turn?"

"No, Sheila, my fierce warrior human, you should relax while you can and let me nurture you. You sit, I'll be back in a flash."

Sheila smiled and watched as the tiny woman skillfully wove her way through the busy mess hall, filled two trays with food she chose carefully, then returned. "Still watching my nutrition, I see, yet still managing to bring my favorites. Ernel, what are we doing here?"

"Excuse me?"

"You and I, what are we doing?"

"Having breakfast?"

"Don't play dumb with me, woman. You know darn well what I mean."

"All right, Sheila. Please don't be upset with me."

"I'm not upset, dear friend, just wondering where your thoughts are, if they mesh with mine."

"Oh, what's on your mind?"

"Ah, ah, ah, I asked you first."

Ernel laughed, a sweet lilting sound that brought a smile to everyone who heard it. "Very well then, I'll confess. I'm nurturing you, it's what I do, what I enjoy, one of the things I miss most about the loss of Ovron. He always did the important things, and I nurtured him, tried to provide peaceful interludes where he could rest and recharge his energy.

"Sheila, getting the chance to do these things for you has returned a big piece of my true self to me, brought me back to the joy I take in life. I could sense the need in you for this, and it gives me great pleasure to do it for you. Please let me continue."

"I'd actually forgotten what it was like to have someone truly care for me, it's been so long. Ernel, it gives me a thrill each time you do it, and I'll mourn bitterly when it stops."

"Stops? It'll never stop, woman; I'm just getting warmed up."

Sheila's laugh of delight brought a smile to Ernel's face. "Ernel, you'll have me spoiled rotten."

"That's the plan."

"Why?"

"Because you need it, and I need to do it."

"So, I come back to it, what are we doing here?"

Ernel laid down her fork and gazed into Sheila's eyes. "I'm not exactly certain, but I like it. For me it began as an exercise in making a friend. I nurture my friends, try to make sure they know I care about them, it's what I do. However, it seems to be going beyond that for me. I don't know why or how, but I'm truly enjoying it and would love to explore the possibilities further."

"Oh yeah, the possibilities are endless."

Ernel sat back, her eyes wide, her mouth forming a perfect O, and color rising in her cheeks. It took a moment to notice the tiny grin of mischief on Sheila's face. "Sheila Singh, I can't believe you did that."

Sheila feigned innocence. "Did what?"

"Teased me when I was trying to be serious. Is this your true nature finally rising to the surface?"

Fighting back the grin, Sheila responded. "Sorry, afraid so."

"Thank the spirits for that," smiled Ernel, as she laced her fingers together and rested her chin on them, batting her eyelashes and trying to look cute.

It was Sheila's turn to have color rise to her face. "Stop it, Ernel. You can't be making a ship's captain blush in public."

"Back to your original question, Sheila, I believe we began building a friendship, but it seems to be evolving into more. I'd love to explore the idea of a relationship with you further, if you're willing."

Sheila sighed and smiled. "Ernel, this is so very different for me. You show affection and concern for me as a person as well as a possible lover. I like that.

"Yes, my darling girl, by all means, let us explore further. I was just afraid it was different for you, that this was just the way the Earalith showed friendship, nothing more."

Ernel reached across the table to take Sheila's hands in her own. "No, it's more, my lady captain, much more, and for the first time, I'm feeling complete again, myself again, and it's you doing this for me. So, as SUVI 20 says, do I get a new title?"

"What title would you like?"

"Sheila's girl?"

Sheila gently squeezed the hands in hers. "Yes, my girl, you can have that title, and I'd be proud to have you claim it."

"Then you have to go to work, and I must abandon you for a short time," smiled Ernel. "My lady captain has asked me to see the new star system with her. I need to make myself presentable before I'm introduced to her crew." She rose, gathered the trays, and hurried away.

* * * * *

"Ship's crew all aboard and ship is ready to launch, Captain Singh."

"Thank you, First Officer."

"Shall I give the order, Captain?"

"Not yet, Commander White, and wipe that grin off your face. We're waiting for a VIP passenger."

"Anyone I know?"

"Hal, I hear they're looking for recruits in Sanitation. Keep this up and I'll put in a good word for you."

"Shutting up now," grinned Hal, as he cringed away from her.

Sheila sighed and stepped outside the ship to see Ernel coming toward her. Sheila sucked in her breath, for Ernel had used her artistic touch to apply her make-up and outfit. This was what an Earalithian woman of the nobility would have looked like for a special excursion, and she was exquisite.

"You like it?"

Sheila found her voice and smiled. "You're completely dazzling and exceptionally beautiful. Come, my lady love, I'll introduce you to the crew."

She took Ernel by the hand and led her onto the ship. "Attention all hands, this woman is Ernel of Reacher, a truly gifted artist, and my companion of choice. She will accompany us today as an interested observer and my guest."

Ernel beamed her delight as she was introduced to each member of the crew.

* * * * *

Sensors on Reacher had found nothing in the system that would indicate advanced technology, now Retriever sped through the system double checking and looking behind some of the larger planets while Reacher turned her sensors outward.

Aboard the Retriever, Ernel stayed back out of the way, but kept her eyes on the forward screen, constantly making notes on the tablet in her hand. Sheila beamed at her proudly as she stole glances at eager artist at work. At length they contacted the Reacher with the go ahead.

"Retriever calling Reacher."

"Sorenson here. What's the good word, Sheila?"

"All clear, Admiral. Nothing but us moving around out here."

"Good to know. Take your time on the way back, you know, do some sightseeing."

"Thank you, Admiral, I'll do just that," grinned Sheila. She turned from the comms to see Ernel smiling wistfully. "What is it, my girl?"

"I was just thinking how amazing it would be to go outside and see it firsthand."

"Forgive me, Captain, but my space suit should fit Lady Ernel," said the woman on sensors.

"Delightful idea, Tagora, and thank you. How about it, my love, want to go outside and gaze at the stars with me?"

"Oh, you know I do."

It took a few minutes to get suited up and into the airlock, but Ernel was trembling with excitement as the outer door opened and she could see the entire star system. Sheila took her hand and together they stepped out and floated away from the ship until the tether lines gently stopped them.

"Are you all right, Ernel? You haven't said a word."

"I'm fine, I'm just trying to commit it all to memory. This is utterly amazing, and it's giving me so many ideas for projects. I can never thank you enough for this."

"Oh, I'm sure you'll think of something."

"Don't distract me now, sweet Sheila, save that naughtiness for later when I get you home."

* * * * *

While Ernel was getting her spacewalk, EX2 left the Reacher and sped toward the lone planet in the goldilocks zone. Ka'Ron stood beside the sensors, hoping against hope that he might see the remains of his people's ship, perhaps even evidence that they had made repairs and moved on, or at least some sign that they had survived.

"Entering atmosphere, Captain Drake."

"Begin standard search pattern, Three."

"Aye, Captain."

"Thirteen, anything interesting on sensors?"

"Water, water, everywhere, Captain, nothing more so far."

"Lilly, hearing anything on comms?"

"Nothing, Captain."

"All right. That darn cloud cover sure is thick."

"There's a break up ahead, Captain. Picking up land formations."

"Slow us down a bit, Three, let's get a good look at her."

"Aye, Captain."

They flew their standard search for hours and saw mostly water with a few islands, before they found the large land mass. At first it was covered with jungle growth, but as they proceeded, they found more open plains, and eventually northern boreal forests.

Lilly was itching to go down and start taking samples. "Patience, Lilly, patience," chuckled Amanda Drake. "Tommy, how's the air down there?"

"Doesn't look all that great, Captain," replied the ship's medic as he focused on his instruments.

"Oh?"

"It's really rich in oxygen. We can breathe it, but everybody will get high for a while until we adjust to it."

"Probably what Earth was like before the industrial revolution," said Lilly.

"Will we need breathing filters?"

"Couldn't hurt, Captain," replied the medic. "I've got some here designed to filter toxins out of the air. A few adjustments should let me damp down the oxy a bit."

"Do it, Tommy. We don't want Thirteen getting all happy go lucky on us."

"I don't know, sounds like that could be fun," grinned Connie, the new security officer.

SUVI 13 just chuckled at their teasing. "Officer Kim, are you suggesting I should be first off the ship to test out the possibilities of the air?"

"Oh no, as security officer, that's my job, but you can come along, you know, keep me company."

"Settle down, people, we've still got a lot of grid lines to cover before anyone does a walkabout."

"Yes, Captain," grinned Thirteen, winking at Connie.

"EX2 to Reacher."

"Jeannie here, go ahead, Mandy."

"We've found lots of water, plenty of land, a variety of climates, lots of animal activity, but nothing more so far, Jeannie. "Settling down for the night. We'll pick it up in the morning."

"Sleep well, sweet Mandy."

The alarm sounded through the small ship bringing a number of groans from the crew. "Rise and shine, people," said Amanda, as she stepped out of her booth and yawned. "Let's grab a few rations then get back to it. If we can finish the grid search today, then maybe Thirteen can take Connie for a walk in the moonlight before next sleep period." That brought a round of laughter as Thirteen just grinned and shook his head.

The meal finished; the ship dropped out of orbit to resume her inspection of the planet. Nervously, Ka'Ron watched the sensors. An hour later his shout told them he'd found something. "There!"

"All stop."

"All stop, aye."

"What is it Ka'Ron?"

"The ship, and more. Life signs, hundreds of life signs." Everyone was trying to get a look over his shoulder.

"All right, step back, people. Ka'Ron, put it up on the big screen." The screen flickered to life, and they saw an aerial view of a large community, people rushing out to stare at the sky. "Thirteen, are you seeing what I'm seeing?"

"Huts, not large buildings, beasts of burden, not machines, leather armor, not metals, spears etc. I'd say we have a fairly primitive society down there."

"Agreed. Lilly, are you picking up any chatter on comms?"

"Nothing, Captain, and no response to hails."

"Okay. Ka'Ron, that crashed ship is yours?"

"Yes, Captain Drake, that ship was one of ours, the Kreenon, our sister ship, the one that escaped. Obviously they made it this far then had to set her down here. It also looks as though there were survivors, but that was long ago, and their descendants have lost their grasp of advanced technology."

"So, are we going down, Captain?" asked Connie Kim.

"Not yet."

"Contacting the Reacher?"

"Not yet. Ka'Ron, do you detect any signs of activity aboard the ship?"

"A couple of life signs, but the ship itself is dead."

"No live weapons?"

"None, Captain."

"Good to know. Three, resume search pattern."

"Resuming grid inspection, aye," came the chuckling reply.

"I don't understand," Connie mused softly as the captain resumed her seat at co-pilot.

"The captain won't go down until she gets the go ahead from the Reacher, and she won't report in until we've gathered all possible information first," replied Thirteen. Connie nodded her head, the captain was a cautious and careful woman, that was reassuring.

As the day wore on they found two more settlements, none more advanced than the first, but both far larger. The vast forests seemed endless and that explained the oxygen rich atmosphere. They also found evidence of an abandoned civilization that nature had slowly reclaimed. There were ruins aplenty along the slowly winding rivers.

Eventually they finished and the ship rose above the planet to a low orbit. The captain called the Reacher. "EX2 to Reacher, come in Reacher."

"Reacher here, EX2. One moment, the admiral is on her way." A moment later Jeannie's smiling face appeared on the screen. "Mandy, what's the good word?"

"I've got lots of good words for you, Suvi-jean. First, Ka'Ron's people did make it this far. We found their ship crashed on the planet. We also found the descendants of the survivors. They've spread out over a large section of the main continent but have regressed to a pre-industrial society. We also found the remains of an older civilization.

"There are also large tracts of land uninhabited. I'd like to go down so Lilly can gather some samples before she chews my arm off."

"Did you make contact with the people down there?"

"No, not yet. We tried with comms, but I don't believe they have that technology."

"All right, Mandy. I'll send Linsey to join you when you make contact. Be extremely careful, Mandy; take no chances."

"I won't, Jeannie. I'll take Lilly down to fill her crates in a remote spot, save the meet and greet for when Linsey gets here. EX2 out."

Chapter 13

It Was Too Easy

While Commander Peters was filling her crates with samples of the vegetation, three Morar stood on the bridge of the downed ship, gazing at the flashing light on the panel. "What does it mean?" asked one. "You are the elder priest, tell us what it means?"

"This spoke to us in the Elder Language," replied the old one leaning on a walking stick. He pushed the fur back from his eyes then continued. "As I understand it, it was one of the ancestors trying to communicate with us, or rather with the ancestors who came to Tarion on the magic ship from the stars."

"You truly believe this? You think the star people have returned?"

"You saw the thing in sky as clearly as I. It appeared then the ship of the gods awakened and spoke. The others went away and now the ancient ship lies quiet once again, yet awake and aware, listening."

"So, what does it all mean?" asked the third Morar, a large female wearing brightly colored leathers and a feathered headdress.

"It means the ancients have returned to us as foretold. If they come alone, they bring joy and prosperity, if the demons followed them through the barrier, then they bring death and despair. You are chieftain, Wel'lyn. It is for you to decide what we do next."

She turned from the elder priest to the young warrior beside her. "Ba'Sha, send runners to the Dota and the Leste, tell them what has happened, tell them to come with their wisest advisors. We must prepare for both eventualities."

* * * * *

While the people on the ground began to prepare for whatever was to come, and Lilly finally filled the last of her crates, Admiral Sorenson sought out SUVI 18. She found her with Linsey in their office. "So, you came to us, Five, then you feel it too."

"I do, Eighteen. Can you tell me anything?"

"I could be completely wrong, but ..."

"Yes, and I could be completely human, but we both know better than that. Tell me, Eighteen. What do you sense coming?"

"The Wrax."

"The Wrax? We destroyed their ship, how could they ... but we didn't though, did we? We crippled it but didn't destroy it. Dammit anyway." Jeannie grabbed her comm unit. "All senior staff to the bridge. Bridge, recall all small ships ASAP. Go to full alert."

She sighed as she let her arm fall back to her side. "Eighteen, how long have we got?"

"Three days is my best guess, maybe more, but I wouldn't count on it."

"Nor will I. Eighteen, once again I am in awe of your abilities, my sister. Come, ladies, to the briefing room with me."

* * * * *

EX2 was already on her way back to Reacher. Retriever was still far away, her captain and companion outside on another spacewalk, when Sheila got the call on her comms. "Captain Singh, sorry to cut short your sightseeing, but Reacher has recalled us home, all possible speed."

"Bring us in, Hal." The tether lines pulled tight, and the two space-suited figures were gently reeled in. As soon as the inner hatch hissed open the ship leaped away toward the Reacher and home. "Hal, any idea what's going on?" asked Sheila as she helped Ernel out of the suit.

"None, Captain. We were just ordered home, all possible speed. The admiral will be waiting in her briefing room. Something must have gone sideways in a hurry."

"No doubt about that. We're on our way, so stay on full alert until we get home. Ernel, I'm so sorry to cut short your excursion."

"No, no, Sheila, it's fine. This has been the most excitement I've had in years, and I can't wait to get back into my studio. I have so many ideas."

Sheila smiled at the bright-eyed woman then hugged her and kissed the top of her head. A few hours later they entered the cargo bay of the Reacher.

* * * * *

"Looks like we're all here, Admiral."

"Thank you, Brandon. People, we have an impending situation on our hands. I awakened this morning with a strong sense of danger approaching. I checked in with SUVI 18 and she agreed. She also believes the danger will come from the Wrax."

"But, how is that possible, we destroyed it, didn't we?" asked Amanda.

"Not quite," replied Jeannie as she paced about the room, her eyes glowing amber. "That ship was already disabled, and we dealt it a major blow, but we didn't destroy it."

"But their engines were already destroyed, beyond repair," said Captain Baris.

"Were they? Here's what we know for certain. That ship was badly damaged and had been in orbit for many centuries. Its warriors periodically awakened, destroyed whatever had caused them to be awakened, and then returned to cryo sleep, awaiting a repair ship.

"Those warriors always returned to the sleeping pods, until now. Why? I believe it was because Ka'Ron was on the bridge flipping switches, so the warriors believed the captain was alive and in control. With no new orders forthcoming they simply went with standard protocols."

"And then we took him away," sighed Brandon Hoffman. "Without orders from the bridge, and the ship wide open instead of closed off as before, they were free to explore and discover the deception."

"Yes," replied Jeannie. "That leaves three possible scenarios. One, they affected partial repairs, enough to follow us here, two, a repair ship did reach them, or three, a new war ship got tossed through the rift.

"No matter which one is the case, I don't want to remain here to face them in open battle. Reacher isn't a war ship, she's a floating home. Yes we have some defenses, but I have no illusions about our chances against a ship built for war. Emmet, how soon can we move on?"

"If all ships are back aboard, we can be ready to set sail in less than an hour, Admiral."

"Wait, wait, what about those people down on the planet?"

"They aren't my people, Grandfather, not my responsibility, the people aboard the Reacher are."

"But they're Ka'Ron's people. We brought him here to find them, and, inadvertently, brought their doom upon them by doing so."

"Are you suggesting we stay here and fight?"

"No, I don't know, Jeannie. Is there no way to help them, nothing we can do at all?"

Jeannie started pacing again, her eyes amber. "Captain Drake, how many people did you see down there, roughly?"

"A few thousands, maybe more."

"All right then, they are familiar with the planet, the terrain, and they outnumber the Wrax, or so we believe. Linsey, take Ka'Ron down there, but don't land. Transport him down to warn them but keep a lock on him. At the first sign of trouble, transport him out and get back here."

"On my way, Admiral," said Linsey as she and Eighteen rose and hurried away.

"All right, Brandon, what are the odds we'll be facing a full war ship?"

"The odds are strong against it, Admiral. There were ships there from a dozen areas, arriving centuries apart, and only one of each. I'd say we're facing the remnants of what we encountered before. Without

Ka'Ron's restraining hand, they must have salvaged an engine somewhere and come after us.

"As true warriors, that beating we gave them would rankle. They've probably come looking for our hides. I'd say there's fewer than a hundred of them, but we have no idea of their capabilities."

"Sheila, how are Brandon's numbers?"

"I'd say he's good on their numbers. Those small fighter ships looked seriously tough though."

Again Jeannie paced. "Emmet, how long does it take for the big gun to recharge?"

"Ten minutes, give or take."

"Moira, can we cut that time down?"

"I could probably shave a minute or two off it, Admiral, what are you thinking?"

Jeannie turned back to face them, and they shuddered. Her eyes were nearly red, and they spoke of a fury none would willingly face. Amanda gulped and sat very still. She had asked for the warrior SUVI, and this was it, Jeannie Sorenson had gone to full battle mode.

"I'm thinking I don't want to spend the rest of my life looking over my shoulder. As an ancestor of mine once said, never leave a live and vengeful enemy behind you. We know they're coming, but I doubt they know that. I'd like to place the Reacher beside that big planet out near the edge of the system, and as soon as they appear, blow them to hell and back.

"I'd also like to have Retriever, EX2, plus Friendship 1 and Friendship 2 fully manned and ready to fight as well. All we've got on the Reacher is the big gun, and we're not as maneuverable as the smaller ships. If we miss a few of them on the first salvo we'll have to deploy everything we have that will fly and can shoot.

"Jake, work with the captains, make sure they have the people they need on those ships."

"Forgive me, Admiral, but those ships already have the best crews on them," said Jake. "However, I believe EX4 is about ready for test flights, and she's built tougher than the rest."

"He's right there, Jeannie," said Moira. "You said to make EX4 a fighter ship, so we did. Harlan's installing the last of the weapons right now."

"According to Eighteen we have two more days. Get that ship into space. Jake, EX4 will be assigned to Security. Take command and man it with the best we've got." With a visible effort Jeannie regained a measure of control and her eyes slowly faded to amber then back to green. "We have two days, people, but I'd rather be ready and in position by end of shift tomorrow. Dismissed."

* * * * *

As the meeting broke up Sheila hurried off to the mess hall to find Ernel, but she'd barely arrived when Jake White joined them. "Forgive me, Ernel," smiled Jake, "But I need the captain's advice."

"Oh, what's on your mind, Jake?"

"You know damn well what's on my mind. Jeannie told me to man the new fighter and crack a crew together. Hell, everyone I'd turn to for this crew is already on somebody else's ship. Who would you recommend for this?"

"Seriously? Jake, this isn't that hard, steal a pilot somewhere, take C crew, and get that ship in the air."

"C crew?"

"Jake, you led them when the riot almost broke out, you led them when Jeannie went to straighten out the passengers, you led them when you rounded up those criminals we sent into exile."

"I was hoping to leave them with Rhonda. I need somebody I can trust to watch Jeannie's back."

"I'll assume that task for you, Jake," said Brandon Hoffman as he joined them. "You're taking C crew on your new ship?"

"Looks like," he sighed in reply.

"They won't let you down, Jake. Go on now, make the admiral proud."

"And don't piss her off. Jesus, I've never seen her like that before, scared the crap out of me."

"You and me both," chuckled Brandon. "Look, if you like, I'll ask Nineteen to go assist Rhonda while you're off the ship."

"That would be great, nobody will give her a hassle with Nineteen there. Okay, I'm good. See you later folks." With that he was up and gone, talking on his comms as he went.

Jake arrived at the new ship to find Commander Moira Duncan there as well as SUVI 2 and SUVI 12. "What's going on?" he asked, as his crew began to arrive at a run.

Moira grinned as she answered. "I'm just here to familiarize you with your new ship. I have no idea what these two characters want."

"We're both SUVI hunters," grinned Twelve as she patted the huge blaster at her side. "Five said you're going hunting, we thought we'd tag along."

"Jeannie sent you?"

"She did."

"Thank the gods for that. You two are on guns. Okay, Commander Duncan, show us the toys."

They were halfway through the tour when an older man appeared at the hatch. "Commander White, I'm Conley Graves, you asked to see me?"

"I did, Mr. Graves. According to your sheet, you were a fighter pilot back on Earth before you signed on for the colony."

"That's right. I developed a problem with my vision and was grounded. Three years into the trip and the ship's doc fixed my eyes, but by then I was committed to the colony, no way to turn back. Not a lot of call for a pilot in the caverns."

"So you're a bit rusty," grinned Jake.

"Fair to say. So, what's going on?"

"This is a new ship, a fighter ship, and there's an enemy due here in two days. I need a pilot; you have two days to blow off the rust."

"What? Are you crazy? I haven't sat in the pilot's chair or anything like it for nearly thirty years, and I'm old, too old. Get one of the SUVI to do it, they've got lightning fast reflexes."

"That's why I want them on guns. Look me in the eye and tell me you don't want to do this."

"Well, I ..."

"Go on, just sit in the seat, see how it feels."

"You know damn well if I do that you'll never get me out of it."

"That's the plan," grinned Jake.

"All right, Commander, if that's what you want. Are you sure you know what you're doing?"

"Nope, just making it up as I go along, picking the best people for the jobs so they can make me look good to the admiral."

Conley chuckled at that. Shaking his head, he moved to the pilot's seat and settled in. Jake winked at Moira as a slow grin of delight crept across Conley's face. "Are we ready for test flights, Moira?"

"Yes, she's ready to go. I'll just head back to Engineering, keep an eye on the readings."

"Chicken."

"You know it," chuckled Moira, as she headed out the hatch.

"Tal, seal her up."

"Hatch is sealed, Commander."

"Conley, request launch clearance then take us out into free space."

"Aye, Commander."

Jake grinned as he listened to his new pilot. The years fell away, and old practices reclaimed Conley. "Reacher, this is EX4 requesting launch clearance."

"You are clear to go, EX4."

The launch was a little bumpy as Conley felt out the controls but soon smoothed out. Everything was much as he remembered from his days in a fighter plane. "We've cleared the Reacher, Commander."

"Very good, Pilot. SUVI 2 rear guns, SUVI 12, forward guns, Ellen, sensors, Moran, comms, Albert, engineering station, Eddy medical, Patel and Ivan, ammo and supplies. Everybody grab onto something and hang on. All right, Pilot, put her through her paces."

"Commander?"

"Look, we'll have to ride this thing in a battle, and we've only got two days to get used to the way she moves at speed. Now do it."

"Aye sir, testing ship's responses now."

It was a wild ride, and one man lost his stomach contents, but all in all Jake was pleased. He was grinning as the call came in from the Reacher, it was the admiral. "Reacher to EX4, come in EX4."

"EX4 here, Admiral."

"We've been watching you on sensors, Jake. Who's flying that ship?"

"The man's name is Conley Graves."

"I know that name. He's a grounder, isn't he? How did you find him and why did you choose him?"

"I'm always reading the files on every person on the Reacher, looking for people who might be able to help us. I knew Conley had been a test pilot on old Earth, so I called him up."

"Well done, big brother. How'd the ship perform?"

"The ship is amazing, Jeannie, but the two gunners you sent me are pouting because there was nothing to shoot at."

"So, go find them something to practice on. Reacher out."

"Conley, you heard the woman," grinned Jake, "keep up the speed and maneuvers, but find a few rocks for the hunters to shoot at."

"Hunting and shooting, aye," came the grinning reply.

Two hours, three free floating rocks of varying sizes, and a small comet later they returned to the Reacher. Jake was grinning with delight. "Well done crew, these are your posts for the coming emergency, but I want everybody familiar with every station on this ship. SUVI, you folks are amazing. I can't order you to ..."

"Hold, Commander," smiled SUVI 2. "On this ship we're part of the crew, and as such subject to your orders. We have no issues here."

"Two?"

"Five trusts you completely, and so will we. We're crew, equal to the rest, and no more. Agreed?"

"Agreed, my friends, agreed, and thank you."

"Commander, that was the most fun I've had in decades," said Conley, "but there's a problem."

"Oh?"

"Commander, I'm game here, but I'm old and we both know this job calls for younger faster reflexes."

"Conley, why do I think you've got something in mind here?"

"Because I do. It's my granddaughter. She's nineteen, bored to tears, has fast reflexes, and spends all her waking hours in VR games."

"Virtual reality games, wha ...? Oh, I get it, she's playing old fighter pilot games, right?"

"She'd be good, Commander. I could train her myself."

Jake thought for a moment then sighed. "All right, Conley, here's the deal. The girl signs on for Security, passes the training, and Sub-Commander Moore's assessment, and then I'll post her to EX4. You stay on as pilot until this entire crew agrees she's ready.

"This is a fighter ship, everyone here has faced combat in one form or another, all are experienced. If we're to risk ourselves to a newbie, I want every member of the crew to be confident in her abilities. Deal?"

"Deal, Commander. I'll talk to her tonight; she'll be at Security first thing in the morning, or I'll never mention it again."

"Deal," said Jake. "Okay, people, get some food and rest, we'll go back at it in two hours."

* * * * *

While Jake and crew were testing out their new ship, Ka'Ron was on the ground. He appeared in a flash of light beside the downed ship, holding his arms wide to show he was unarmed. Several people came rushing toward him with spears at the ready, but they stopped when they saw he was weeping.

An elderly Morar approached carefully. When he spoke, the translation unit at Ka'Ron's chest spoke the words so Ka'Ron could understand. "Who are you? Are you one of the ancestors? Why do you weep?"

"My name is Ka'Ron of Morar Three, Ka'Sensa Clan. I am, was, second officer on a ship like this one. I knew many of the people who flew this ship. I weep with joy to know they survived, and I weep to see my own people once again, for I had long since given up hope of ever seeing another Morar face."

The elder waved off the spears. "Why have you come to us at this time? Do the death dealers follow behind you?"

"They do, but they are not as many as they once were. I have friends in the sky, and they will fight the bringers of death, but I fear for them. Over the centuries I have watched the Wrax obliterate so many."

"Is there no hope at all, Ancestor?"

Ka'Ron drew a deep breath and straightened up, brushing the fur back from his eyes. "There is, for my friends have defeated the Wrax once before, pushed them back then escaped them. However, the Wrax have followed us here, a feat we didn't believe possible.

"Those few Wrax who remain are not the many they once were. Our friends will diminish their numbers further, but should any of the Wrax reach the ground, you must be ready."

"What should we do?"

"Flee into the forests, hide in caverns, choose the terrain yourselves; do not try to fight them in the open. Hide so they must leave their ships to reach you, then strike from hiding and strike in numbers. Even the weak can overcome the strong if there are enough of them.

"If you will permit me, I'll remain here with you. Perhaps there are weapons aboard this ship that we can use, other ways to defend ourselves."

"Will you tell me how you have remained alive for so long, Ancestor?"

"I was sent aboard the Wrax ship to destroy it from within. Success came, but not entirely, and I was trapped there. There is a way to sleep in a frozen state for long periods of time, and so I did. Awake for only short periods then many years of sleep. Each time the alarms sounded I awakened to watch helplessly while the Wrax destroyed yet another people.

"Eventually I was rescued by those who brought me here. Sadly, in so doing they awakened the Wrax. Now, my people, will you tell me why there are so few of you after all this time?"

The old priest sighed and leaned heavily on his walking stick. "At first the people flourished, great cities were built, then came the plagues that destroyed most of us. This planet, this home, will not tolerate a large population of any species, and so we returned to a simpler way of life, to live in harmony with the world that supports us. We tightly control our population."

"That is true wisdom. So now I ask for sanctuary, will you let me stay, help you against the dealers of death who hunt us all?"

"Ancestor Ka'Ron, you are welcome to stay, but the rest is not my decision to make. I've already sent for the leaders of the three clans, together they will decide, but I will champion your cause. As the elder priest, my word will carry influence."

"Thank you. I will now contact my friends above to let them know I'll be staying here." He reached for the comm unit at his shoulder. "Ka'Ron to Linsey."

"Linsey here, everything okay down there?"

"All is well, Linsey. Go back to your people now, I will remain here with mine."

"As you wish. Good luck, my friend."

Chapter #14

Preparing for War

Sheila Singh stood gazing into the eyes of her Earalithian girlfriend. "Ernel, I'm so sorry about all this."

"All this?"

"First your tour was cut short, then everybody aboard the Reacher joined us for breakfast, and ..."

Ernel's sweet lilting laughter stopped her. "Dear Sheila, there is no need to apologize. I had an exciting time on the tour, made my first spacewalk, I met many of the people who govern our small world at breakfast, and all in all, I've enjoyed it.

"The idea that there's an enemy coming to attack us is disturbing, but that was always a possibility on the colony as well. Nothing new there, not for me. So, now you have to rush off to work, and I need to get into my studio. Come for me when the shift ends and you're ready for a meal. I'll have our space ready by then."

"Our space?"

"The quarters, my studio. Sheila, with the possibility of impending doom looming over us I'm not willing to engage in the idea of a long courtship. You go to work and then return to me, that is, if you ..."

Sheila stopped her with a kiss. "I'll be back here as soon as I possibly can get loose. Don't forget me while I'm gone."

"How could I ever forget you, Sheila Singh," sighed Ernel, as Sheila disappeared around a corner. Smiling to herself, Ernel went inside and set to work.

Sheila arrived at her ship to find the admiral and the rest of the captains waiting for her. Jeannie grinned, Amanda chuckled, and Sheila blushed. "What's going on, friends and family?"

"We're going for a ride in Linsey's ship," replied Jeannie. "Look, the reality here is, there's only one person I know of with firsthand knowledge of a battle in space."

"Ka'Ron," sighed Linsey, "and I left him on the surface."

"You did right, Linsey," replied Jeannie. "You left him with his people at his own request. However, now we need his expertise, so we must go to him, and we have little time. Contact him as soon as we're in open space, ask him to confer with us."

"Understood, Admiral. Please, board the ship and we'll get a move on."

They followed Linsey onto the ship and settled in as she took the captain's chair. "Ship is sealed and ready for launch," came the voice of the ship's AI.

"Thank you, Ship. Ettelan?"

"We're cleared for launch, Captain Linsey."

"Take us out, Pilot, then return to where we left Ka'Ron, all possible speed."

"Aye, Captain. Launching." The ship rose up and moved swiftly through the open bay doors, then rocketed away. While they were in flight, Linsey contacted Ka'Ron and set up the meeting. Within a few minutes they were back in low orbit above the old crashed ship, Ka'Ron and others were waiting.

"Admiral Sorenson to Ka'Ron, please respond."

"Here, Admiral. How can I be of service?"

"Are you ready confer with us? We have great need of your knowledge of the Wrax."

"I am here with the council of chieftains and the Elder Priest. You will be welcomed here."

SUVI 18 stepped forward to grip Jeannie by the arm. "Don't go down there, Five."

"Eighteen?"

"I trust Ka'Ron, but not the others. It feels all wrong."

"Then we bring them here. Linsey, can you transport them all here simultaneously?"

"We can, Admiral. Eighteen?"

"Working," replied Eighteen as she stepped to the transport controls. A few moments later there was a flash of light and five Morar appeared on the transport pad.

"Forgive me, Ka'Ron, but there's no time and I'm in a hurry. Tell us about the tactics of the Wrax. When they come, what will they do, how will they attack, what are their preferred tactics?"

Before he could answer Eighteen stepped up to the chieftain wearing the brightest headdress. "Your desire and planned attempt to capture one of us has failed. You will be returned to the surface unharmed."

The creature looked as though it might attack her, but she made a motion with her hand and in an instant the intruder was returned to the surface. "It's now safe to continue, Admiral."

"Thank you, Eighteen. Now, Ka'Ron, when the Wrax attack, how will that attack manifest? What will they do first, next, and so on?"

The tightly controlled power exuded by this person frightened the Morar, including Ka'Ron. "Admiral, first the main ship will fire upon you, doing irreparable damage. While the main weapon recharges they will deploy the small fighter ships. They cannot do as much damage, but they will concentrate on the weakened areas of your ship and any small ships you may deploy. Their favored tactic is to swarm the opponent. Once the main weapon is ready, they will scatter until after it is fired."

"How long will that take?"

"Roughly ten minutes of time for the weapon to recharge."

"Good to know. What are the weaknesses of the smaller ships?"

"There is only one that I am aware of. They are vulnerable from behind, but there were few who could get behind one. Once the engines were blown, and they retreated to the big ship, a number of the small ships were brought down or destroyed from behind. There's nothing more I can tell you, Admiral."

"You've been more than helpful, Ka'Ron, and I thank you for it. You may return with us, or we can return you to the ground with these people."

"I would prefer to return with my people, Admiral."

"Do you believe it safe for you to do so?"

"The ancestor will not be harmed, Leader of the Sky People," said a tall female. "As chieftain of the largest clan, I promise you this."

"Then I wish you well. Send these people home now."

Eighteen guided them onto the transport pads then signaled the Earalith man at the controls. They vanished in a flash of light to reappear where they were standing before they were taken.

"That was foolish," said Ka'Ron, as he faced the man who'd been sent back. "You nearly alienated the only ally we have with a hope of defeating the death dealers. Elder Priest, give this man your impressions of the admiral."

"The ancient is right," said the old priest, as he leaned heavily on his staff. "That one exudes a tightly controlled power, a fury none would willingly face. Her strength is beyond us, and you could never have held her for ransom. The knowledge you seek to gain is already here. That mighty leader came to our very own ancient for advice.

"Think about that. If so powerful a leader comes to Ka'Ron for knowledge, why would we not listen to him?" The other stood shamefaced under the disapproving gaze of the other chiefs and the elder priest. He didn't respond, so the elder priest went on.

"Ka'Ron, what will happen now?"

"The Wrax that come will not be the mighty slayers of old, but few in numbers and weakened. With luck, the Admiral will defeat them in the sky. If any manage to reach the surface we'll fight, as we already agreed."

"And once they are defeated?" asked the tall female chieftain.

"Then the Admiral will come to us for trade, food stuffs, minerals from the ground, and anything still useful or functional on the old ship."

"No, they cannot defile the ship, that which brought our ancestors safely to Tarion. We will defend it to the death."

"How, Wel'Lyn," sighed Ka'Ron. "You saw how easily they took us from the courtyard. No, our best chance is to trade fairly with them. Much of what is on the old ship will be of no use to them, more they can study and learn from without disturbing anything. What few bits they might want to take they'll replace with better, I'm certain.

"Now we must prepare for battle against the Wrax, not our allies, and we must pray our allies don't abandon us in our time of need."

"What do you mean?" asked the elder priest.

"The admiral and that other one, are SUVI. The SUVI are superior beings, they know things before you think them, and they are terribly powerful. If the Admiral grows angry, or distrusting, of the Morar for that attempt to capture her, they might abandon us to our fate."

"They would do that?"

"Why would they not? She called to confer with us in good faith, and one of us plotted betrayal. Your own ancestors abandoned the rest of our people and fled here. Had they remained to fight, who knows, the Wrax could have been destroyed long ago. However, none of that matters now. Now we prepare to face the Wrax alone. If we don't have to, so much the better."

The elder priest and the others nodded their agreement.

* * * * *

While Ka'Ron was delivering the hard news to the Morar, Friendship landed lightly in the cargo bay of Reacher. Jeannie stepped to Eighteen and gave the smaller woman a gentle hug. "That was well done, my sister, and I thank you for it."

"You didn't know, Five?"

"I felt something wrong, that I shouldn't trust the Morar, but we needed the information. No, I wasn't aware one of them would try to capture us. Come, people, to the briefing room for a council of war." As she strode toward the hatch, she reached for her comm. "All senior staff and captains to the briefing room."

* * * * *

The first officer glanced around the room then spoke. "Looks like everybody's here, Admiral."

"Thank you, Brandon. Jake, you've brought a guest."

"I'm here as acting captain of EX4, Admiral. This woman is Rhonda Moore, my second-in-command of security and she's here as acting Security Chief."

Jeannie smiled at that. "Yes, and rightly so. Welcome, Sub-Commander Moore. Report."

"A lot of unease aboard the Reacher, Admiral, but no real issues. SUVI Nineteen is acting as my aide during the current crisis, and has mad skills at calming folks down."

"Excellent, thank you. Brandon, is the ship ready for battle?"

"As ready as can be, Admiral. Engineering has toughened up the shields, looked for and beefed up any weaknesses, plus shaved three minutes off the recharge time of the main cannon. Rhonda will tighten up Security so there's not likely to be any distractions from within during the crisis. I'd say we're as ready as we can be."

Jeannie nodded her head, her eyes glowing amber. She rose and began pacing about. "Captains, can I safely assume your ships are battle ready?"

"All ready and secure," came several replied.

"Good. Olga, your two salvage ships aren't fighters, but you do have shields. When we launch the fighters I want you to launch as well. Stay back behind Reacher's shields but be out there and visible. I want to show the Wrax as many opponents as possible.

"We spoke with Ka'Ron, and he informed us they will begin with their main weapon aboard the big ship. I don't plan to give them that chance. Emmet, as soon as they get within range, fire the main cannon.

"We'll hide Reacher behind that gas giant. With luck we'll catch them by surprise and destroy them on the first salvo. That's the way a SUVI hunter brings down a garog. If we fail to fully destroy them with the first shot, the small ships will launch, but stay back behind Reacher's shields. Even if we fail to completely obliterate them with the first shot, we should have time for a second before the small ships have to engage their fighters.

"Now then, captains, has anyone any ideas about what tactics you'd like to use against their fighter ships?"

"I do, Admiral."

"Go ahead, Jake."

"Admiral, Ka'Ron said they're vulnerable from behind. If they deploy the fighters, I'll take EX4 around the gas giant and hit them from behind. That'll pull them back around to face me, and the others can then get at them from the weak side."

"I like it, Jake. I'll go with you."

"Jeannie?"

"At that point in the battle, I'll be aboard Friendship Two with a small crew of SUVI. We'll hunt at your side against these garog." Jake nodded, so she went on, her eyes a deep amber. "Does anyone else have anything to add?"

"I do," grinned her grandfather.

Jeannie turned to him then relaxed, matching his grin. "Captain Baris?"

"Admiral, you said you'll be taking out Friendship Two. That little ship has served us in a number of ways, but as yet has no real designated purpose. May I suggest he be commissioned as the Admiral's personal ship?"

Jeannie thought about it for a moment. "Yes, I like it, Grandfather. He will be my personal fighter ship. When time and materials permit, I'd like to see his shields and weapons beefed up as much as possible."

"Jeannie?"

"Grandfather, I highly doubt the Wrax will be the last aggressors we face. In future, I'd like to see us far better prepared, but for now we do what we can. So, now we have a plan of action. Captains, return to your ships and prepare your people. Brandon, you'll be in command of the Reacher when I leave the bridge for my fighter.

"Linsey, take me down to Friendship Two and introduce me. Meeting adjourned, people, prepare."

* * * * *

They entered the small Earalithian ship with Linsey leading the way. "Ship welcomes Captain da Silva and Admiral Sorenson."

"We greet you, Ship," replied Linsey.

"How is Ship to serve this day?"

"Ship, today you receive a new designation and title," grinned Linsey. "I now pass over command to Admiral Sorenson."

"Ship is honored to accept Admiral Sorenson's command. Standing ready to receive orders, Admiral."

"Thank you, Ship. Your new designation is SUVI F1, SUVI Fighter One. You will be my personal fighter ship. Know that this crew will all be SUVI. We are physically stronger than humans or Earalith, and thus can survive greater accelerations and faster course changes."

"Understood, Admiral. Ship will access SUVI attributes from files of Reacher and adjust accordingly. Are we going into battle?"

"Possibly soon, F1. For today I want to familiarize the crew with your weapons and abilities. F1, have you ever been in a battle before?"

"Thirty-seven times, Admiral. Shall I familiarize you will Earalithian battle tactics?"

"Yes, do so for the entire crew, if you please."

"Step to the learning station, Admiral." Jeannie stepped up and Linsey helped her into the strange cap. Jeannie sucked in her breath as her vision blurred then she was in the midst of a battle. After a few moments she was able to see the bigger picture, follow the tactics as applied from both sides, and also see how the Earalith managed to outwit and defeat their opponents.

After about an hour it stopped, and she removed the helmet. "Well, that was enlightening. I now see why Morthel insisted we avoid any possibility of encountering the Earalith Empire. These folks were not to be messed with.

"Nine, you'll be my second aboard this ship, and command if I'm incapacitated or absent."

"Very good, Five."

"I'll return to the bridge of Reacher now. Nine, learn the battle tactics, see that the rest of the crew does as well, then assign the crew positions."

"Aye, Admiral Sorenson," he grinned. She gave his shoulder a gentle squeeze then walked away.

* * * * *

Moira Duncan looked up to see the admiral stride into Engineering. She set aside her task and rose to greet her. "Jeannie? You look like you're on a mission."

"I've just received an education in Earalith battle tactics. I'm surprised that Earalith ship didn't finish the Wrax when they first met."

"I'd say the Earalith ship was finished off by the rift, Jeannie. I saw the wreck, and I doubt she could have flown or fought. We got extremely lucky there, we came through without any real damage."

"Well, here's hoping our luck holds. I need to know what our ships are capable of, speed and maneuverability wise."

"Jeannie, it's a bit late to be making changes to the ships now ..."

"No, no, Moira, I don't want you to make changes, I just need to know what they can do. I now know what the two Earalith scouts are capable of, but it's our ships that concern me."

"EX2, Retriever, and EX4 will match or exceed any maneuvers the scouts can perform. Dorind has a keen eye for design, and he worked closely with me on these ships. They'll stand up, Jeannie, I promise you that."

"Good to know. All right, Moira, I'll stop fussing and go back to the bridge." Moira grinned at her retreating form.

* * * * *

Rhonda Moore stood gazing at the room as it slowly filled up with her security forces. When all were present, she stepped forward to address them. "For those of you who might not know, I'm Sub-Commander Rhonda Moore, and for the next day or so I'm in command of Security. People, we're in a unique situation right now and for the next few days. Reacher is expecting to be attacked.

"Commander White has assumed command of a new fighter ship assigned to Security by Admiral Sorenson. Commander White and his crew will see the main action. We have a different mandate.

"Until the current crisis has passed, vital areas of the Reacher must remain free of passersby and/or curious people. They must be kept clear so the people who work there can perform their duties unhindered. That's our task, keep the passengers restricted to passenger areas and away from the ship's vital systems.

"This won't be as easy as it sounds, you'll have to be firm, but patient. Explain to any you encounter that they're being turned away for the safety of the ship. They should go to their elected officials if they have concerns.

"If you have issues or concerns, you bring them to me ... after the crisis is over, not before." Rhonda sighed and let her shoulders sag. "I mean it, people, no rough stuff unless there's no other choice, but we must maintain order so the bridge crews and vital systems can work unhindered. Get some rest, tomorrow could be an exciting day."

As she stepped down from the podium she saw a dejected looking girl walking away. She caught the girl's eye and beaconed her over. "Who are you and how did you manage to get into this meeting?"

"I'm sorry, I didn't mean to intrude. My grandfather told me to be here first thing to sign up for Security training. I was here but they sent me away."

"So you came back?"

"Five times."

Rhonda grinned at that. "Then you'd be Ebony Graves; Jake told me you'd be coming. Look, we're up to our ears in it for the next day or so. If we survive that, see me in my office and I'll personally get you started. Deal?"

"Deal. Oh, ma'am, I can't thank you enough for this."

"Go on now, scoot and stay out of trouble for a few days."

"Yes, ma'am," grinned the girl, as she turned and fled, a bright smile on her face.

Rhonda reached her office door to find a tall man waiting for her. "Marcus, what's on your mind?"

"I want to reactivate, at least for the short term."

"Why should I do that, you were pretty adamant about taking early retirement?"

"Look, Rhonda, my personal life, or lack thereof, isn't the point here, nor is it any of your business. The new ships have been cherry picking this department for crews, and now you're short-handed when you most need experienced people. I'm ready to come back for a few days until this mess gets settled, and then I'll happily return to my retirement."

She sighed and gazed at the ceiling for a moment then returned her attention to him. "Yeah, I can't deny any of that. All right, start of shift tomorrow, suit up and take your old post at the brig. Quiet there right now, but I expect it'll liven up once things get going."

He nodded and started away. "Marcus." He turned to give her a questioning look. "Thanks." He nodded then walked away.

Rhonda entered the office and flopped into her chair. Nineteen eased himself into a chair facing her. "You're surprised I took him back, aren't you, Nineteen."

"A bit," he chuckled.

"Ah, he was right, my friend, we do need him, he's a fully trained and experienced security officer, and he's good at the job. Man had a mid-life crisis, hooked up with a firebrand of a woman, got competitive with her, and got his ass kicked. He took his wounded ego, and his toys, then left the playground. That doesn't mean he's not good at his job, doesn't mean he can't do the job anymore, and we do need him, at least for the moment."

Nineteen smiled as he nodded his head in agreement. "And the girl?"

"Jake's pet project," smiled Rhonda. "Jake found an Old Earth fighter pilot among the grounders, dug him out and put him to work. That's all shiny and fun in the short term, but the man is old. This gal is that man's granddaughter, spends all her time in VR games playing fighter pilot. Jake wants her trained for security then as pilot for the new ship. Long term problem solved."

Nineteen looked thoughtful. "I understand the need for a backup pilot, but why the security training?"

"Come on, Nineteen, you've hung out with Jake enough to guess that one."

"He wants her to develop the discipline needed for a pilot under fire. He wants her ready to obey orders without questioning them."

"Right as rain, Brother SUVI, right as rain." Nineteen chuckled again and passed her a container of water.

* * * * *

They were ready to settle down for the night, but Suvi-jean was still pacing. Amanda sighed and stepped into her path. "Jeannie, my love, please stop fussing and try to relax. You've done everything you could and more. Relax and rest now, there'll be time enough for action tomorrow."

"If they come tomorrow."

"Would it be a bad thing if they don't?"

"Yes."

"Why, lover? Why would it be bad? Wouldn't another day to prepare be a good thing?"

Jeannie sighed and reached to pull Amanda tightly to her. "Yes and no. Yes, the additional time to prepare would be good, and yet, if it takes too long the stress will wear on our people, they could get lax, and …"

Amanda had stopped her with a kiss, deepening it until she felt Jeannie's knees begin to shake. "You're just fussing now. Come to bed with me and I'll see what I can do to take your mind off your troubles."

"I don't know, Mandy, I'm pretty wound up. It could …" Amanda kissed her again. A groan of delight came from her throat as Jeannie pulled her tight for the kiss then swept her up in strong arms and tossed her on the bed. With a feline grace she shed her clothes and crawled up beside Amanda, who had a grin on her face.

Chapter #15

First the Calm

Sheila Singh sighed with delight as she opened her eyes to find Ernel sleeping with her head pillowed on her shoulder. As Sheila stirred, Ernel murmured then stretched, sat up and beamed her brightest smile. "Good morning, my super ship's captain, did you sleep well?"

"I did indeed," replied Sheila, matching Ernel's smile. "I have to confess, sweet lady, last night was my first time ..."

"With an alien?"

"Hey now, I didn't say ..."

"It's all right, Sheila, it was my first time with an alien too."

That made Sheila laugh. She hugged the smaller woman to her and kissed her hair. "Brat. I was trying to say it was my first time with a woman."

"Yeah, mine too. Ovron always said girls are the best, now I know what he meant."

Again Sheila laughed. "Well you're in a playful mood, are you always so cheerful first thing in the morning?"

"Always start the day with a smile and words of love, that's my new motto. I love you, Sheila Singh."

"And I love you, Ernel, my darling girl. So tell me, are you trying to keep my mind off my troubles this morning?"

"Yes I am," smiled Ernel and she snuggled closer, "is it working?"

"Perfectly," replied Sheila, then the alarm sounded. "Computer, silence alarm." It stopped instantly. "Well, that's my cue to rise and shine. Shall we get going and have breakfast before I rush off to work?"

"Let's do, I'll go first." With that Ernel leapt from the bed, tossed the covers over Sheila's head then raced to the facilities.

Sheila let out a yelp of surprise as the bedcovers settled over her. Ernel looked up from her seat on the throne to see a smiling Sheila shake an admonishing finger at her. "I warmed the seat for you," she grinned.

"You're too good to me," sighed Sheila, as she settled down to relieve the pressure in her bladder.

Still gently teasing each other, they swiftly prepared for the day then marched off to the mess hall for breakfast.

They arrived to see many of the other crews already there, chatting quietly among themselves. There was an air of expectation that was almost palpable. Glancing about, Sheila could see the tight shoulders of the various commanders and captains. Realizing what she was seeing, she became aware her own shoulders were tight.

Ernel reached across the table to grip her hand and squeeze. "It will all be fine, my love."

"Are you so sure?"

"I am. Of all the billions of people in our combined species, we few are the lone survivors. I have always believed in a higher power, and I do now. We few have survived for a reason, whatever it may be, but I can't believe that reason is to be slaughtered by the Wrax. No, my most cherished, the Wrax will come, and they will be defeated."

"Ernel, thank you for that."

"You're welcome, my love. Now, off to work with you, I'll take care of this." With a gentle squeeze of her lover's hand, Sheila was up and away, headed for her ship. She wanted to double check that everything was ready as could be.

* * * * *

Jake stepped aboard the ship to find the crew already at their stations. "Bunch of eager beavers," he grumbled, as he took the captain's seat. There was a round of chuckles at that. Jake was grinning with pride. "All right, report."

"Ship is secure and ready, Commander," came the reply from behind him. "Munitions are topped up, weapons are loaded and ready, shields are charged to full capacity, and so is the fuel."

"Perfect. Pilot?"

"Ship is ready, Commander, and so is the pilot," came his reply. "Awaiting orders to launch."

Jake sighed and relaxed his tall frame into the seat. "Now that brings us to the day's agenda. People, we now invoke the age-old military tradition, hurry up and wait. There's nothing more we can do until the enemy shows up, which they may or may not do today."

"What happens if they don't come today, do we go home and hope they'll wait until tomorrow before showing up?"

"No, we stay right where we are. We do not leave this ship until after the crisis has passed. EX4 will be fully crewed and ready the instant the Wrax show up, no matter when that happens. If they stall all day we'll sleep in shifts, some of us always awake in case we need to launch in a hurry."

"Is that what the other captains are doing?" asked another voice.

"They'd better be, or the admiral will skin 'em alive. That's what the crew of the Reacher will be doing. Might as well relax for now." There were a few chuckles as the crew found comfortable seats.

* * * * *

Aboard the other ships it was the same. "Captain Drake, are we really going into a battle?"

"Yes, Lilly, we are. I know you're scared, so am I, all of us. We're explorers, not warriors, but this time we're the prey. We're being hunted, and it's up to us to ensure our own survival.

"The admiral has fully familiarized herself with Earalithian battle techniques and strategies. She has a plan, and we're a part of that plan. With any luck it won't come to it, but if it does, we'll be ready, ready to defend ourselves and our combined people."

"Of course you're right, Captain. Sorry."

"Relax, Lilly, we're all wound up over this, and if you're like me, you wish the Wrax would hurry up and get here. Sadly, we can only sit here and wait for them to arrive."

"And fuss?" grinned Thirteen.

"Yes, Thirteen, and fuss. I'll take my own advice now and try to relax."

*　*　*　*　*

Captain Singh reached her ship to find the last of her crew arriving. SUVI 20 was being hurried along by Sessas as Sheila stood by the hatch. "Stop for an extra cuddle with the chief medical officer, did you Twenty?"

Twenty chuckled as she confessed. "Busted. So why are you running late, a last snuggle with a famous artist maybe?"

"Shut up and get to your station, Twenty."

"Aye, Captain, shutting up now."

"I wish. Hal, are we all ready?"

"Now that the gunners have finally arrived, we're ready as can be, Captain."

"Shut up, Hal," grumbled Twenty.

They could easily hear Sessas' hissing laughter. Sheila smiled as she settled into her chair. Her crew was ready. Of all the crews, this was the only crew to have seen anything close to actual combat. She was fully confident in their ability to function under fire. They were ready, now came the hard part, waiting for the enemy to arrive.

Chapter #16

And Then the Storm

It was six hours into the shift when the alarm sounded. Jeannie was on the bridge, pacing, when she heard the voice of the woman on sensors. "Got something on sensors, coming in fast. Looks like it could be a comet."

Before Jeannie could respond her comms pinged. "SUVI 20 to Admiral Sorenson."

"Sorenson here. What's up, Twenty."

"They're here."

"We've got something on sensors that looks like a comet, but nothing more."

"It's not a comet."

Jeannie turned to the Second Officer. "Emmet, target that object and fire."

"Guns."

"Locked on target, weapon is fully charged, Commander."

"Fire."

"Weapon fired."

"Anita, what have you got?"

"Sensors show comet destroyed, Admiral. One large piece still inbound."

"Target that, fire the weapon as soon as possible."

"Admiral, several smaller objects are breaking away from that chunk, all changing to intercept course with us."

"Crap, the bastards hitched a ride on a comet. Battle stations, battle stations. Launch all small fighters. Brandon, the Reacher is yours." With that Jeannie fled the bridge and raced to the launch bay and her waiting ship.

Brandon Hoffman sighed as he watched her go, then he turned back to the big forward screen. "Anita, are they spreading out any?"

"Not yet, Commander, and they're coming in a lot slower now without the aid of the comet."

"I see, thank you. Gunner, target those incoming fighters as best you can. As soon as the weapon is ready, fire."

"Aye, sir, weapon will reach maximum charge in thirty seconds. Maintaining lock."

"How many of them are there, Anita."

"I make it sixty-three, Sir."

"Weapon fully charged in three, two, one, ... Weapon has fired. Recharging."

"Very good, gunner. Sensors, results?"

"I see eighteen left, Commander. They've scattered now."

"Hoffman to Sorenson."

"Here."

"We've thinned them out, Admiral, but you'll have at least eighteen to contend with. Good luck."

"Thank you, Commander. As soon as we're clear, put your shields to max until it's over."

"Understood. Hoffman out. Ready at shields, on my mark go to full shields."

"Aye, sir."

"Small ships are away, Commander, all clear, salvage ships remaining within main shields."

"Raise shields."

"Shields at full, Commander."

"Now we wait. Emmet, can you fire the main cannon out through the shields?"

"Don't believe so, Commander."

"All right, we do this the hard way. Gunner, when the weapon is fully charged, lock onto one of those small Wrax ships then let me know."

"Aye, sir."

"Emmet, when he's ready, drop the shields, fire the weapon, then get the shields back up. We'll have to be fast and precise on this people. Stay sharp."

"Weapon ready in three, two, one ... I have a lock."

"Drop shields."

"Shields are down."

"Fire."

"Target destroyed."

"Shields!"

"Shields back to max, Commander. Reacher unharmed."

"Good to know. How did we do, Anita?"

"That shot took two more of them, Commander."

"Very good. Sadly, they'll be looking for that next time. We won't dare drop our shields again."

Suddenly his comms came alive, it was Jeannie. "Brandon, what the hell ...?"

"Got two more, Admiral. You're down to sixteen now."

"Thank you, Brandon, but don't do it again, they'll be watching for it."

"Understood, Admiral, maintaining shields." He was grinning and the bridge crew all gave a nervous chuckle at that. The first officer was cool under fire and that gave the bridge crew a sense of confidence. They began to relax somewhat, more hopeful than before.

* * * * *

Aboard the smaller ships, Jeannie was issuing orders over the comms. "Sorenson to all captains. Tease them in people, Jake and I'll circle the planet and take them from behind. When they turn to attack us, that's when you hit them with all you've got. Fight hard and good luck, my brothers and sisters." With that her comm went silent. F1 and EX4 sped away, circling the planet.

EX2, Friendship, and Retriever moved away from Reacher, slowly easing to a position that would force the incoming Wrax to expose their backs to F1 and EX4. "Drake to Captain Singh."

"Sheila here."

"Sheila, you're the most experienced captain, how do you want to do this?"

"They've got the numbers on us, Amanda, so we'll have to play it fast. It's a lot harder to hit a moving target, so we wait until they're almost on us then we jump to full speed. Our job is mainly to entertain them until the admiral hits them from behind, then we get serious.

"When they turn to fight F1 and EX4, then we attack like we mean it. I'll lead, you two stay on my wing until it all goes crazy."

"Understood. Lead on." Amanda looked around to see her crew at their stations, ready. "Thirteen, you're on forward guns?"

"Set and ready, Captain."

"Connie, you on the tail gun?"

"Locked and loaded, Captain Drake."

"Mr. Sacumbtu, you guys ready?"

"We each have a full canister of sealant ready, Captain."

"Ready on medical, Captain."

"Shields."

"Shields at full, Captain."

"All right, folks, here we go. Three, keep us on Retriever's wing as best you can."

"Aye, Captain."

Sheila's voice sounded over the comms then Retriever leapt toward the approaching Wrax fighters. EX2 and Friendship were close behind. Suddenly five of the Wrax closed in and opened fire. Retriever returned fire and one Wrax ship exploded, but Retriever's energy shields were stripped away. The next shot shut down her engines.

EX2 was doing better. The lightning fast reflexes of the SUVI pilot kept her from being hit, and she managed to disable two of the Wrax.

Friendship accounted for two more of the Wrax before F1 and EX4 arrived. It was clear Linsey's Earalith ship and crew had seen combat before.

Aboard Retriever all appeared chaos, but it wasn't. Sheila was shouting orders and the crew sped about their tasks. "Hal, get those fires out, Ellen, we need those engines back online now. Kumar help her. Twenty, Sessas, keep those buggers off us, we're sitting ducks right now."

EX2 and Friendship were protecting Retriever as best they could, but the rest of the Wrax were converging on them, aiming for the wounded Retriever. As they neared their prey they were suddenly hit from behind. Two ships exploded and two more were hit. The Wrax turned to fight this new enemy.

As the Wrax turned, EX2 and Friendship attacked from behind. The sixteen Wrax ships were now down to seven, then EX2 spun out of control, a gaping wound in her side. "Mayday, mayday, EX2 calling for transport extraction. Reacher, do you copy?"

"Reacher here. Hold EX2. We can't lower our shields until it's over. Hold."

"Negative. We have wounded and we're leaking atmo. Request immediate extraction."

"Negative, EX2. Hold."

Suddenly a new voice was heard on comms, it was Rhonda. "Transport, do you have a lock."

"Transport locked and standing ready."

"Shields are down, Commander Hoffman."

Brandon Hoffman turned to see Rhonda standing at the control panel, her eyes hard as flint and SUVI 19 right at her side. "What the hell, get ..."

"Transport now."

"Transporting. Second transport successful, Sub-Commander."

Rhonda flipped the switch, then let her arm fall away from her shoulder.

"Shields are back at max, Commander Hoffman."

Brandon gave Rhonda a hard look, but she didn't flinch. "Do you have any idea what you just did?"

"I know, and I accept the consequences. Transport, did you get them all?"

"We got them all, Sub-Commander. Captain Drake and Mr. Sacumbtu were transported directly to medical."

"Thank you, Transport." Rhonda turned back to Brandon, took off her insignia and passed it to him.

"Keep it, we'll discuss this later." With that he turned back to the main screen.

Outside the battle raged on. Retriever had regained enough engines to limp back toward the Reacher, Friendship was taking a pounding until EX4 came to her rescue, but it was F1 who was drawing the Wrax attention. Somehow that ship was able to twist and turn at alarming rates. Moreover, he could fire his weapons accurately at those speeds. Who or what could be flying that ship?

As another Wrax ship exploded under combined fire of Friendship and F1, the last two Wrax turned and fled toward the planet. EX4 managed to catch up and kill one, but the other reached the planet and disappeared into the forests. Jake called Ka'Ron with the warning then turned back to the Reacher.

Chapter #17

Aftermath

Jeannie was already back aboard Reacher, running to the bridge. "Brandon, report."

"Reacher unharmed, Admiral. EX2 is badly damaged, as was Retriever. Friendship and EX4 report minor damage, as did you."

"Casualties?"

"None that I'm aware of right now, Admiral."

"Good to know. Sorenson to Medical."

"Here, Jeannie. We've got the crew of EX2 here. I've stabilized the worst injuries, we lost Mr. Sacumbtu and Kristof, Thirteen will recover in a few days and Mandy should make a full recovery."

"Amanda?"

"She's stable, and sleeping, Jeannie. I've sealed the wounds, soothed the burns, but the broken leg will need time to heal."

Jeannie sighed with relief. "Thank you, Carla. Were there any other injuries from the other ships?"

"A few bumps and bruises from Retriever, Captain Singh has a gash on her arm, and Kumar got a nasty burn, but we've got that. I'll have a full report for you soon."

"Then I'll let you work. Sorenson out. Sorenson to Engineering."

"Moira here."

"How bad is it?"

"Recovery One has EX2 under tow, so I'll know more soon. Recovery Two has just landed Retriever and we're looking her over now."

"All right, Moira, I'll leave you to it. Sorenson to Security, report."

"Sub-Commander Moore here. All's quiet, Admiral."

"Good to know, Sorenson out. Now, Brandon, how did she hold up?"

"The shields were strong, Admiral, but those weapons were powerful. We'd never have stood up to a full battleship."

Jeannie nodded thoughtfully. "So, now tell me what you don't want to tell me."

"I don't want to tell you that. As long as I don't say anything it doesn't matter."

"Fine, then off the record, tell me. I need to know, Brandon."

"All right, Jeannie. We had a minor mutiny during the battle," sighed Brandon.

"Oh? Rhonda didn't mention anything."

"Rhonda was the mutineer."

"What???"

"You gave orders not to lower the shields again. When EX2 called for extraction I asked them to hold. They said they couldn't hold, but I refused to drop the shields.

"I heard Rhonda behind me asking Transport if they had a lock. When they confirmed she dropped the shields until Transport gave the all-clear then she raised them again. SUVI 19 was with her, acting like a bodyguard."

"I see."

"By rights she should face a court martial."

"But?"

"Jeannie, she did what I wanted to do, what I should've done. She made a command decision under enemy fire and saved a lot of lives. Jeannie, this is your call. What do you want to do here?"

"Nothing right now. I want to get the Reacher fixed up, get our people back in action, get our ships repaired, and we've lost people who must be properly honored with ceremony. Once all that's under control, I'll decide what to do with our mutineer.

"Right now I'm headed for Medical, you have the bridge."

Jeannie entered the medical bay and Carla appeared before her immediately. "She's still sleeping, Jeannie. She'll be okay. The burns on her face responded well. They weren't deep and the sealant kept them from getting bad, they won't scar. The one she had on her arm will scar though. The wound on her right leg was deep, and her left was broken, but we sealed the wound and set the leg.

"I've given her something to help her sleep. The wound is responding well, and the stem cells are already repairing the broken leg. She'll need a few weeks to recoup, but she'll make a full recovery. Thirteen's lucky he's got such a hard head. He'll be okay in a day or two."

Carla continued to list the injuries and treatments, but Jeannie's attention drifted away. She could hear Amanda moaning in her sleep, calling her name. Carla rose to go to her, and Jeannie followed, taking a seat beside the bed. She held Amanda's hand and made soothing sounds. Amanda settled down and sighed as she drifted into a deeper sleep. Carla patted Jeannie's shoulder and slipped from the room.

Down in the cargo bay Jake was just climbing down off his ship. "Tidy her up, guys, then head home for some rest. We're done for the day." He turned to catch SUVI 20 in his arms.

"Easy girl, easy, I'm all right, I'm good."

"Oh, Jake, that was so scary."

"Yeah, it was. We came out from behind that planet and saw Retriever floating free, nearly stopped my heart, girl."

"Yeah, those things were tough all right. Thankfully, we carry extra medical on our ship, so everybody got patched up in a hurry."

"Are you okay?"

"I'm good, honey, just a few bumps, nothing major. Sessas got tossed around a bit, but she's okay."

"Hal?"

"Right behind you, big brother, and all good."

"Do either of you know what happened with EX2?"

"They called for extraction, but Commander Hoffman said no," replied Hal. "Suddenly the shields went down, they were transported back to Reacher, then the shields came back up. Nobody seems to know what happened."

"I'll check it out."

"You can do that later. Right now you'll come with me to the mess for a meal, and then we're going home for ten hours sleep," declared Twenty.

"Yes, ma'am," sighed Jake, as he allowed his shoulders to slump. Twenty took his arm and led him toward the mess.

While Jeannie was sitting with the sleeping Amanda, Moira was gazing at the damage to EX2 and Retriever. Dorind was beside her. "We have much work to do, Commander Moira."

"Indeed we do, my friend, indeed we do. Dorind, you know what we have to do here."

"Improve the designs, make the weak points stronger, improve the shields, and more."

"Yes, and the weapons, we need more effective weapons. Why does it always come to this? All we want is to be left in peace to survive, but ..."

"As such, Moira, we are the prey. All prey simply seeks to survive, to be safe. Better ships with stronger shields and weapons will help ensure that survival. Even prey animals have claws."

"Yes, you're right there. Okay, so let's take a look at where EX2 was hit, and what happened structurally to the metal when that happened. That should give us an idea of how we can make improvements." With that, they set to work.

* * * * *

Jeannie was still sitting with Amanda when Jake arrived with Twenty and Carla. "Still sleeping?"

"Yes."

"Jeannie, Jake and I'll stay with her while Twenty takes you to the mess for a meal."

"No, I ..."

"Come, big sister," smiled Twenty, as she gently took Jeannie by the arm and pulled her to her feet. "Come on now, Mamma Twenty will feed you and you'll feel better." Jeannie smiled weakly and allowed herself to be led away.

They entered the mess to find it nearly full, the room abuzz with animated conversations as crew members told their friends and families about the battle. Jeannie sat quietly listening while Twenty brought her food. "Twenty, my sister, your warning saved us all."

"Oh, I ..."

"Yes it did," said Jeannie. "I sensed the danger near, but you knew where it was. As a result of that timely warning, we got off a shot to destroy the comet and thus slow them down. Our second shot all but eliminated them.

"Twenty, there were over sixty of them at the start. Had they all managed to reach us, we could never have survived. As it was, the last sixteen of them nearly made an end of us. You saved us all, my sister. You're the hero of the day."

"No, Jeannie, there are no heroes today, only frightened people desperate to survive. I may have sounded the warning, but you led us to victory. We're SUVI, we do what we do for the greater good, the protection of the people."

Jeannie smiled. "So that's it."

"What?"

"Twenty, I was intrigued by, yet a bit puzzled at your eagerness to join the Retriever's crew. That ship would naturally be used in emergency situations, place the crew in possible danger. We SUVI aren't predators, we're created from prey, a savage and aggressive prey, but prey, nonetheless.

"I see now you hoped to use your talents to lessen the danger to Retriever's crew as well as to serve the greater good."

"Yeah, you got me. I believe my super intuition is a natural extension of a prey animal's survival instincts. I hoped I could use that to our advantage. Seems to work okay."

Jeannie laughed at that and gave the girl's hand a gentle squeeze. That laugh helped release the tension from her shoulders and she relaxed at last. "All right, Twenty, I'm ready to go back now. You need to take Jake home for some rest and Carla has work to do."

"And you need to be with Amanda. Okay, let's go." She rose easily and swept up the trays then returned them. Falling into step with Jeannie, she accompanied her back to medical.

As they entered the medical bay, they heard Connie gently chiding Thirteen. "No, you're not fine, you have to stay there until the medics say you can go."

"Says who?"

"Says me, now you lie back and rest."

"I'm SUVI, I don't have to take orders from you or anybody else." Connie's sweet laughter brought a smile to everyone who heard it.

"Okay, okay, give me a minute here, let me rephrase that. You're SUVI 13, Captain Drake's go-to guy, the main protector of the EX2 crew, Admiral Sorenson's advisor and mentor, my teacher and friend. We all depend on you and need you at your best. Therefore, for the greater good, you have to lie back and rest."

Thirteen sighed and relented, grudgingly. "Using SUVI psychology on a wounded man is cruel. You're a mean woman."

"You like me."

"Like you? Why would I like you?"

"Because I'm as cantankerous as you are?"

He laughed heartily at that then sighed as he reached for her hand. "That could be it all right." Jeannie smiled and went in to sit beside Amanda.

All through the medical bay it was the same, friends and lovers of the wounded warriors sitting with and trying to cheer up the injured.

For three days the Reacher hung still in the heavens, the crews of the small ships tried to tidy them up, stood by fussing as the Engineering crews worked on the repairs, and Reacher's bridge crew searched the surface of the planet for the one remaining Wrax ship they couldn't account for. On the third day there was a ceremony to honor the two men lost in the battle.

The two salvage ships had gathered up as much of the wreckage as they could, and Engineering poured over that as well. They were looking for any tech they could use to improve their own, plus they were trying to understand the weapons, as well as devise a defense against them.

In all that time, Jeannie rarely left Amanda's side, except to officiate at the memorial service. It was late on the third day when a soft groan from the bed jerked Jeannie out of a sound sleep. "Mandy? Mandy, are you awake? Oh thank the gods you've returned to me."

"Jeannie? How did, wait, I'm on the Reacher, aren't I?"

"Yes, my love, you're in medical."

"Did we win?"

"We did," chuckled Jeannie.

"My crew, is ...?"

"The survivors of your crew are all fit and ready for duty, Captain Drake, however, you'll need a few more days to recover before you go back into action."

"Survivors? Jeannie?"

"Carla was unable to save Mr. Sacumbtu and his second, Kristof, they were too badly burned. Thirteen is now ready for duty again and Morthel has been acting as captain in your absence."

"Morthel? Thirteen wouldn't do it?"

"Connie wouldn't let him. Our mentor seems to be a bit henpecked these days." That made Amanda chuckle. She choked a bit and Jeannie held a container of water so she could drink.

"Well, somebody's awake at last, I see," smiled Carla, as she peeked in. "All right, Admiral, you have a ship to see to, and I need to check out our favorite patient. Go on, Jeannie, back to work with you."

"Yes, ma'am," sighed Jeannie, as she stood and stretched. "I'll come back in a little while, Mandy." With that, she kissed Amanda on the top of the head then stepped out and headed for the bridge.

"Admiral on the bridge."

"As you were, people. Brandon, how are we doing?"

"We're getting ourselves patched up, Admiral. Reacher is fine, we got through it all unscathed. Both salvage ships were also unharmed, but they've been busy since the shooting stopped.

"EX2 is being put back together and will return to service soon, Retriever's engines have been repaired and she's ready for service. Friendship and SUVI F1 took minimal damage and have been fully repaired. EX4 has a few more scrapes to be patched up, but she came through without any real damage.

"The shields are still up and we're remaining on alert status as ordered."

"Excellent."

"So, have you given any thought to what you want to do with the mutineer?"

Jeannie sighed and let her shoulders sag. "Are you making a formal complaint?"

"I'm making a request," he replied.

"Oh? What do you think I should do with her?"

"I think you should give her my job and accept my request for retirement."

Jeannie sighed as she gazed at her friend. "Denied. Brandon, I need you at first officer, I depend on you more than you know."

"Jeannie, I failed you, and that young woman didn't. She was cool as can be, fully understood what was needed, what that would cost her if she did it, then she calmly did it anyway. She'll make you a far better first officer."

"Maybe in another ten years, but at the moment I need you right where you are. Request denied. Now, if you're not going to make a formal complaint, I have no official knowledge of any incident in my absence, and therefore have no reason to take any action for any reason against anyone who hasn't been officially mentioned. Correct?"

She was grinning, and he shook his head ruefully. "Jeannie ..."

"Remember when I ran off to save Grandfather and Amanda took control of the situation? I tried to step down, but none of you would let me. You all said things like this happen, that no one has all the right answers all the time. Brandon, my friend, this was one of those times."

"I guess," he sighed. She patted his shoulder then left the bridge.

Brandon looked over to see Emmet Jones grinning at him. "Told you." Brandon just chuckled and nodded.

Jeannie checked in on Amanda again, then sought out Jake in his office. Jake already knew of the incident; Rhonda had told him. He was greatly relieved to know she wouldn't face any repercussions for her actions. He also knew Jeannie had something on her mind, but he didn't ask.

Her next stop was to seek out her grandfather in his quarters. "What's on your mind, Jeannie?" he asked, as he passed her a container of water and indicated she should sit. He sat facing her and waited patiently for her to organize her thoughts.

"Grandfather, during that battle there was an incident on the bridge. EX2 was damaged, her crew wounded, some gravely, and they were calling for emergency extraction. In the heat of battle, I'd told Brandon to keep the shields up no matter what, and so, he refused to lower them for the transport.

"Rhonda Moore, acting chief of security, was on the bridge at the time. She quietly told Transport to stand by, lowered the shields, ordered the transport, then popped the shields back up. The whole process took less than a minute, and as a result, the Reacher was exposed for that minute, but several people were saved as well.

"The young woman knew the cost to herself, but she also knew what had to be done, and she did it. Nineteen was beside her and he described her in action. She confirmed Transport was ready, watched the forward screen, when the Wrax were all momentarily turned away she dropped the shields and gave the order. The shields were back up before the Wrax were aware."

Frank Baris sat grinning at his granddaughter. "So, now instead of hauling this young mutineer before a court martial, you want to promote her, am I right?"

Jeannie chuckled at that. "You know me too well, Grandfather. Help me here, what do you suggest I do?"

"Jeannie, the people in command of this ship when you came aboard felt we were more than capable of doing what was needed under normal circumstances. Your arrival and the ensuing invasion by the grounders showed us the fallacy of that.

"Since you became captain you shook things up, promoted some unlikely people to positions of authority, and you did it all running on those SUVI instincts of yours. As a result, we've survived a number of situations that would have made an end of us otherwise.

"Look at Carla Marks, for example. Under the traditional model she would never reach her current position for another twenty years or more. Linsey da Silva the same, without you she'd spend the rest of her career as a second-rate engineer.

"Jake White, he was wasting away in Sanitation, now he's the most effective head of Security we've ever had, Brandon will say the same. Amanda as well, she'd never be more than a transportation operator, but now she is one of the most effective captains in our little fleet.

"Jeannie, your instincts haven't let us down yet. Tell me what you want to do here."

"I need a way for Rhonda to step in during an emergency and take command. She's cool under fire and has good instincts. How do I do that? Running the Reacher takes a detail-oriented person, and that's Brandon. The man is amazing at the job, and I'd be lost without him. How can I do that without messing him up, or losing him?"

Frank's grin just widened. "Do you really want to know?"

"Stop teasing, Grandfather. I can see you have the solution, now spill it."

"Promote her to captain of the Reacher."

"What???"

"You're the Admiral, Jeannie, you'll still be in command. Rhonda can leave the day to day running of the ship to Brandon, yet take over in an emergency, or if you're off the ship like you were in the battle.

"I watched that whole battle from the bridge of Recovery Two, and I saw what you were able to do. How did you manage that, by the way? How did you overcome the speeds and turns, because that made all the difference?"

"F1, SUVI Fighter 1, was an Earalith fighter scout. I took a full crew of SUVI with me; we can withstand greater acceleration and faster turns than a human or Earalith. F1 has a lot of prior combat experience as well. That's also why I want Rhonda on the bridge if I ever have to do that again.

"So, Captain of the Reacher, eh?"

"Yes, Admiral. That position has been vacant since you were promoted."

"Thank you, Grandfather. I really wanted a way to make this happen, but I couldn't see how it could work. This will also take a lot of work off my plate, allowing me to focus more on the bigger picture, our overall survival. I like it, I'll go talk to Brandon now."

She was on her way back to the bridge when her voice was heard over the comms. "First officer to the bridge briefing room."

Brandon was waiting for her when she arrived. She told him what she had planned, and he grinned with delight. "Jeannie, once again you amaze me. Gods, how I do love the way your brain works."

"So, you approve?"

"I do, Jeannie, I do. I've watched you promote people out of the blue, and each time they rise well above expectation. I think you've got another winner here. Do it, and I'll do everything in my power to help her succeed, then I'll get the hell out of her way in an emergency."

Jeannie nodded and reached for her comm. "Chief of Security to the bridge. Repeat, Commander Jake White to the bridge."

He arrived a few moments later. "Jeannie, what's up?"

She told him. "Jake, please don't think this is me overlooking you for ..."

"No. Jeannie, my sister, no. Not ever. Look, you already gave me my dream job, I always dreamed of being Chief of Security one day. You gave me that, I'm good at it, and I want to keep it. If Rhonda's shown you the right stuff, if you believe she's the one for the job, then I say go for it."

"All right, Jake. I'll check in with the rest of the senior staff, get their take on it before we jump. Keep it under your hat for now."

"Mum's the word, little sister." He grinned as he left the room.

Two days later she was back in the briefing room with Brandon. "All right, I believe I'm ready, let's get the party started. All senior staff to the bridge. All captains to the bridge."

Amanda was the last to arrive, her leg in a cast and Carla pushing the wheelchair. She grinned and winked at Jeannie, knowing what was coming. "Looks like we're all here, Admiral."

Jeannie nodded then reached for her comm. "Sub-Commander Rhonda Moore to the bridge."

"On my way." That voice sounded nervous, and Jeannie grinned. Rhonda arrived a moment later and swallowed hard as all eyes turned to her. She marched stiffly to the long table, came to attention, and saluted. "Sub-Commander Moore reporting as requested, Admiral."

"Thank you, Rhonda, please be seated. Now, to begin, people, during the recent battle with the Wrax there was an incident on the bridge. That incident has been brought to my attention, and now we must address that issue.

"Sub-Commander Moore, you were involved with that incident, were you not?"

"I was, Admiral."

"And you said at the time that you would accept the consequences of your actions, am I correct?"

Rhonda swallowed hard again. "Correct, Admiral."

"Then, after due investigation and deliberation, I now promote you to the rank of Captain. Captain Moore, the Reacher has been without a captain since I was promoted to Admiral of the Fleet. You are now Captain of the Reacher. Congratulations."

Rhonda had risen to her feet determined to accept whatever punishment came her way. She was having trouble processing what she'd just heard. She stood there, her mouth working, but no sound coming out. Eventually she found her voice. "Are you serious?"

"I am," grinned Jeannie. "The post of Reacher's captain has been vacant for a while. Your actions during the battle clearly demonstrated you're the woman for the job. You calmly took control, watched for an opening, rescued a number of people, then re-established the shields to keep Reacher safe. On the advice of Reacher's first officer, her former captain, and SUVI 19, I now offer you the post of Captain of the Reacher."

Rhonda was still trying to process the sudden turn of events. "I ... I don't know what to say, I ..."

Jake lightly poked her in the ribs. "Say 'thank you, Admiral, I accept the post.'"

With wide eyes she looked at him, saw the grin there, then turned back to Jeannie and swallowed before speaking. "Thank you, Admiral, I accept the post and swear I'll do my utmost to not disappoint you. May we speak in private for a moment?"

Jeannie quirked an eyebrow at her then nodded. "This way." She led Rhonda into her private office. "All right, Rhonda, speak your piece."

"Admiral, I'm thrilled beyond measure to be offered this post."

"But?"

Rhonda let her shoulders sag. "A ship can have only one captain, ma'am. If you do this, Reacher becomes my ship, the crew becomes my crew. You command the fleet, but I command the Reacher. If you continue to go about as usual, I'll be no more than a …"

"Whoa, whoa, Rhonda, I know. Trust me, I know full well what you're saying. I learned that the hard way when Grandfather's ship got into trouble. I tried to jump the chain of command and Amanda had to, ever so gently, take back control of her ship.

"Rhonda, this whole thing we're trying to do here has too many moving parts, and it's just getting more complex as we add more ships. I'm swiftly reaching overwhelm, and in truth, I'll be more than happy to step back, remain in command of the fleet, but the Reacher will be your ship."

Rhonda nodded slowly. "All right, Admiral, I'll do this for you, and I'll give it my all, but know this, there'll be no hard feelings if it turns out I can't do it and you have to remove me."

"That'll never happen, now, enough of this. Let's go back in there and you start acting like a captain."

Rhonda chuckled at that. "Yes, ma'am."

They walked back into the briefing room together, smiling. Once Rhonda had resumed her seat, Jeannie spoke. "So, once again I offer you command of the Reacher, Captain Moore, do you accept?"

"I accept the post and the honor, Admiral Sorenson. I'll do all in my power not to disappoint."

"You won't disappoint, Captain Moore. Your first officer is a treasure, and he has offered to mentor you in the new position. Sadly, it'll be hard for you as you'll have the admiral looking over your shoulder all the time. I know how that feels as I have the former captain watching my every move." That brought a round of chuckles and Captain Baris shaking a finger at her.

"All right, Captain Moore, get out of here and get into a captain's uniform. Come back to us and we'll make the official announcement for the ship's crew and passengers."

Rhonda was still somewhat in shock, so Jake gently turned her and urged her toward the door. She suddenly came to life and fled the room; she was soon back in a fresh captain's uniform. Jeannie stepped to an open space and beckoned Rhonda to join her. Amanda grinned and flicked a switch as Jeannie nodded.

"Attention all ship's personnel, this is the admiral speaking. Gather round as I will make an important announcement of great interest to all of you." She gave it a moment then went on. "Since I assumed the mantle of admiral, the post of Reacher's captain has remained vacant. As we gain more small ships, it becomes clear to me that post can no longer remain empty.

"Therefore, it gives me great pleasure to present to you, your new captain, Captain Rhonda Moore. Captain Moore, the Reacher is yours." With that Jeannie shook Rhonda's hand then stepped back, leaving Rhonda facing the camera.

"Greetings, crew and passengers, I'm Captain Rhonda Moore. As your new captain, let me assure you nothing has really changed here. Admiral Sorenson is still in command of the fleet, including the Reacher. Crew, if you have concerns, please relay them to your superiors and they in turn will bring them to me.

"Passengers, all policies established by the admiral will remain in place, and I will happily meet with your elected officials to discuss any concerns you may have. In other words, everything is business as usual. Thank you for your attention and I look forward to serving with you all."

Amanda flipped the switch back and the room stood to applaud. Rhonda stood blushing furiously. "So, now what happens?"

Jeannie grinned at her. "Now you have a ship to take command of. Better get to work."

Rhonda chuckled at that. "All right, Admiral. Orders?"

"Hold our position here while we rest and recoup from the battle. We have to complete all repairs, get our respective crews sorted out, then decide what to do next. I want to make doubly sure that last Wrax has been eliminated before we relax our guard.

"Rhonda, I'd like to keep that office we just used for my own use, we can share this room for larger meetings, you'll want to have your first officer find you some more captain-like quarters, but you can't have mine."

"Works for me, Admiral," she grinned.

"All right then, we'll confer later after you've had a chance to settle in. Thank you, good people, I'll take my leave now. Captain Moore, the meeting is yours."

"Thank you, Admiral. I have nothing for the captains, but I'd like a few words with the senior staff."

* * * * *

Once Jeannie and the captains were gone, Rhonda turned to the remaining people. "People, most of you have been in senior staff positions as long as I can remember. You have a wealth of knowledge and experience that I'll need to draw upon regularly. You've worked with one young inexperienced captain, can you do it again?"

Brandon chuckled at that. "Captain, before offering you this position, the admiral conferred with each and every one of us, and, speaking for the senior staff, I tell you we all agreed with her assessment of the situation and approve of her decision.

"Captain, what you did on the bridge that day is exactly what I wanted to do, but I held back as a lifetime of training dictated. You didn't. You were calm, decisive, and took control, watched for an opening, executed a rescue, and then popped the shields back up. I say, in all honesty, should we ever find ourselves in another battle I'll be more than happy to see you on the bridge."

There was a round of agreement from the others, and Rhonda sighed in relief. "Thank you, one and all. I believe Admiral Sorenson was accustomed to using a less formal style than my original training would dictate. I'd like to maintain some of that if we can.

"My first order of business will be to visit each department and learn all I can about how it works and why. I'll also steal SUVI 19 as my personal aide. Sorry, Commander Hoffman, but Nineteen and I work well together."

"And with Nineteen beside you no one will give you a hard time. I like it," chuckled Brandon.

"Anyone who gives me a hard time will soon realize I don't need Nineteen to set them straight, but you're right, with him there it'll stop a lot of foolishness before it starts.

"So, if there's nothing further, we'll meet here again at start of shift day after tomorrow. Hopefully, by then I'll have an idea of what you're talking about when you report."

A round of chuckles and congratulations followed then the meeting broke up. Jake hung back and asked for a word in private. "What's on your mind, Jake?" asked Rhonda, once they were alone.

"I just want you to be clear on something, maybe I should say, I want us to be clear on it. EX4 is assigned to Security, and every time the Admiral goes running off on her ship, I plan to be right behind her in EX4, watching her back."

Rhonda thought for a moment before she replied. When she did, Jake was surprised. "Jake, I know why you watch the admiral's back so carefully, and I know that the most likely place for that to be necessary is on the Reacher, trouble from the grounders.

"Her ship, SUVI F1, is an Earalith scout fighter, and she's manned it with a full crew of SUVI. You and I both know I need you here watching my back more than she does when she's aboard that ship. Jake, I need you here, doing what you do best.

"Of all the senior staff you're the one I'll lean on the most, the one I'll need to help me truly get full control of the Reacher. She couldn't do it without you, and I won't be able to either. You're Chief of Security for Reacher, Jake, and I need your full attention and best efforts there.

"If you can't do that for me, say so right now. The Admiral can promote you to Chief of Security for the Fleet, make you a captain, and you can have EX4. I'll appoint someone else to head up the Reacher's Security."

Jake was stunned and sat back, gazing at her with wide eyes. Finally, he started to grin. "Once again Sister Jeannie works her magic."

"What does that mean?"

"Rhonda, Jeannie has a way of seeing a person's true potential, she promotes people way above expectation, and they always rise to the challenge, excel in spite of themselves. Both Carla and I are prime examples of that.

"How about this, I'll give you all you've asked for and more. I'll find a new second and train them to take over the job should that promotion to fleet ever come, but I won't go looking for that promotion. I promise I'll have your back all the way."

"Accepted, with gratitude, Jake," sighed Rhonda as she relaxed back in her chair. "I'll admit I'm still in shock here, and I'm in way over my head. Any hints on how to rise to the occasion?"

"Yeah, toughen up a bit."

"Jake?"

"You're like Jeannie, open and easy going for the most part until things go all to hell. Pull that back a bit unless you're with trusted and true friends. Do like you just did here with me."

"You bastard, you did that on purpose just to see what I'd do."

Jake chuckled. "Busted."

"So, did I pass the test?"

"You did. Rhonda, you sounded like a true captain, like Jeannie would have under the same circumstances. You'll do just fine, Captain Moore, and I'll do everything I can to help you."

She shook her head and grinned. "Get out of here and go to work, Jake." Smiling, he saluted and left her alone.

The new captain of the Reacher put her head in her hands and sighed. She allowed herself a moment of overwhelm then stood up and straightened her uniform. "Might as well get on with it. My brain is going to hurt by end of shift today." With that thought, she left the room and strode onto the bridge.

Chapter #18

It's Not Over Yet

Amanda laughed with delight as she was swept into strong arms then deposited gently on the bed. Her bandages were off, and she was down to the cast on her leg. "Jeannie sweetie, can you tell me something?"

"What is it, my exquisite companion?"

"I'm still a little surprised at how you gave up the Reacher. I didn't ever think you'd give up that command."

"It comes back to when Grandfather got into trouble, sweet Mandy. You showed me then that I can't do it all, I need people I can trust to help me. The job was getting too big again. There are too many ships to control, too many enemies to fight, too many variables to keep track of. I knew I was going to give up the Reacher, but I didn't know who would be the right one for Captain. You wouldn't take it, I know, Sheila would be good, but she's nearing retirement age.

"I was thinking about asking her to do it in the interim, then Rhonda committed mutiny, saved your life, and demonstrated she has the right stuff and won't wilt under fire. If I can build a good relationship with her the Reacher will be in good hands for years."

"And that stability will reassure the people, give them something familiar to count on, and having a human at the helm will relax them even more. I love the way your SUVI mind works, my warrior woman."

"Oh yeah? Can you see how it's working now?"

"Jeannie, behave. Carla says the treatments are working perfectly and I'll have the cast off in a couple of days. Save some of that badness until I can play too."

* * * * *

Jeannie reached the bridge right behind Emmet Jones. The new captain was already there. Jeannie hung back, smiling as she listened to the conversation.

"Good morning, Captain, you're up early."

"Couldn't sleep, too much on my mind. Relax, Commander Jones, I'm not here to get in your way, I'm here to learn. First off, who's your back-up in case something goes sideways?"

"Anita's on sensors right now, Captain, but she has a strong grasp of every job here, is a pilot in her own right, and I'd feel quite comfortable leaving her in control of the bridge."

"Good to know. Now, I'll reappear often as time and circumstance allow. I'll need you to familiarize me with every station, its function, and more. However, I know Admiral Sorenson left you in charge of the bridge, and I intend to do the same. I just need to be familiar with the working parts."

"Thank you, Captain. I'll do my best to help you."

At that Jeannie grinned and slipped off the bridge. "Yes indeed, the right person for the job." Smiling, she headed for Engineering.

She breezed onto Engineering to find Moira poring over a schematic. "Good morning, Jeannie."

"Good morning, Moira. What's going on, I expected to find you down at the ships, overseeing the repairs."

"Aye, well, I was, but Captain Moore had another task for me."

"Oh, what has she got you doing?"

"The bloody impossible is what it is. She wants more weapons on Reacher, weapons that can shoot out through the energy shields. I told her it can't be done."

Jeannie was grinning. "What did she say to that?"

"She said Linsey da Silva figured out the Earalithian language, did I want her to ask Linsey to do it? Well that just won't do. There's no way in hell I'm letting an entry level engineer at a project like this, we'd all be killed.

"So, tell me you've got something else for me to do."

"Not right now, I don't, Moira. If I come up with something, I'll relay it through your new captain."

"Thank you for that," came Rhonda's voice from behind her. "Do you want me to put the chief engineer back on the repairs?"

"Actually, Captain Moore, I came to ask Moira if she thought there was a way we could devise weapons that could shoot out through the shields," grinned Jeannie. "I see you're well ahead of me on this one. So, want to join me for a walk through the repair bay, or are you on a mission?"

Rhonda started to reply, but the comms interrupted. "Alert status, alert status, captain to the bridge."

"Bridge, this is the captain, what is it?"

"Captain, the Wrax ship has come out of hiding and is devastating a Morar village."

"Understood. Lower the shields. Launch Bay, this is the captain. The instant Admiral Sorenson is ready get those doors open for her. Bridge, as soon as the admiral is away, get the shields back up."

Both stations acknowledged her instructions. Jeannie had called for her SUVI crew to meet her at F1. With a nod of approval to Rhonda, she raced away. Rhonda hurried to the bridge.

"Captain on the bridge."

"As you were. Commander Jones, status?"

"F1 is away and shields have been raised, Captain."

"Excellent. Anita, can we see any of what is going on down there?"

"We can, Captain. I'll put it on the forward screen." They watched as F1 shot towards the surface of the planet.

The Wrax ship rose to meet them, weapons firing as she rose, but the speed of F1's evasive maneuvers prevented any direct hits. F1 suddenly ducked low then came up under the Wrax ship, crashing into it and damaging it badly. As it spun out of control it took a direct hit from F1's weapons and spiraled down to the surface of the planet.

One lone creature crawled out of the wreckage as F1 landed and Jeannie stepped out of the hatch. The creature shook itself then faced her, flexing its slightly clawed hands. It growled something, and the small box attached to her uniform translated for her. "Come meet your doom, scum."

Jeannie waved her crew back then stepped out, pulling a long dagger from her belt. The Wrax whipped up a weapon and fired, but she wasn't there. It fired and missed again; she sped past him, unharmed.

The Wrax spun around to face her again, realizing only then his weapon was gone, it was now in her hand. She tossed it aside and spoke, her machine translating for her. "Don't look now, Wrax, but I think you're wounded."

Slowly the creature's eyes began to register the pain. He looked down to see a great gash in his abdomen. With a snarl of rage he charged at her, slashing with his claws. Again she sped past him, unharmed. He turned to her slowly this time, another wound in his chest. "Not possible," he grunted as he slowly sank to the ground.

She walked toward him, stooping to gather up his weapon. "Utterly possible," she said, then shot him with the weapon. He went limp and lay still.

As it became clear the Wrax was defeated, on the bridge of the Reacher, everyone let out a sigh of relief as Jeannie stood over her fallen enemy. "That, good people, is a sample of what our beloved Admiral is capable of," said Rhonda. "Personally, I'm glad she's on our side."

"Second that," muttered Brandon Hoffman.

Rhonda reached for her comm. "Captain Moore to Captain Volkov."

"Here, Rhonda, what's up?"

"The admiral is down on the surface. I believe she's got another Wrax fighter for you to salvage."

"I'll go down for a look," chuckled Olga Volkov. "Thanks for the heads up."

"Lower the shields, stand down alert status."

"Aye, Captain, shields are lowered. Captain ..."

"You made the right call, Commander Jones, and I thank you for it. Where the safety of the ship is concerned, we err on the side of caution if at all possible."

* * * * *

"Sorenson to Captain Volkov."

"Already on our way down, Admiral. Captain Moore said you might have some salvage for us." Jeannie chuckled at that.

SUVI 9 had come up to stand beside Jeannie. "That thing looks like a small Garog."

"It does at that," she sighed, as she stooped and wiped her blade on the corpse. "We'll wait here until Olga has gathered up the salvage."

Nine looked up to see the Morar coming out of hiding, their spears at the ready. He nodded then gave a piercing whistle. The rest of the SUVI appeared from the ship, all carrying weapons. They fanned out around Jeannie protectively.

Jeannie looked for an obvious leader, then spoke to the one in the elaborate headdress. "We mean you no harm, and we've killed the one who hurt your people. We don't want to fight you."

The tall one in the headdress stopped and lowered her spear. "You are Admiral, friend of Ka'Ron. He said you would come, that we should hide and allow you to destroy the killers. The ancient is wise, we will not fight you." She signaled with her hand and the others reluctantly lowered their weapons.

"Is Ka'Ron near?"

"The ancient and Elder Priest are in the sanctuary under protective guard. The ancient will want to speak with you."

She turned and gestured, a young warrior sped away toward the old downed ship. Recovery One was already on the ground and moving the Wrax ship into her cargo hold by the time Ka'Ron arrived. "Admiral Sorenson, we are deeply in your debt."

"The Wrax are defeated and no longer a danger to you and your people, Ka'Ron. Now we come to the next step."

"The next step?"

"We need some things this planet might provide, there is possibly tech aboard that old ship we might find useful, and more. Will the Morar trade with us?"

Ka'Ron had no need to translate, Linsey's translation device did that as Jeannie spoke. He looked to the chieftain who nodded slightly. "The Morar will negotiate, Admiral. Bring us a list of what you need, and we'll see what we can provide. I fear the Morar will not want to have the temple ship disturbed, but I'll speak to the council on your behalf."

"Thank you, Ka'Ron. I'll send Linsey to negotiate for us, will that be acceptable to you?"

"It will, Admiral."

"Then I see Recovery is on her way home, and so must I be." With that she turned and stepped back onto her ship.

* * * * *

After witnessing the Admiral's demonstration of both her ship and her prowess in combat, Linsey had little difficulty arranging for trade. Oddly enough, it was brightly colored cloth that was most popular. In exchange they got new and different foods, access to a number of minerals that the Morar were just learning how to work, plus permission was given to inspect the ship.

The idea was to inspect, raid the main computer for information, copy out the tech manuals, etc., but remove nothing. A week later it was done. Jeannie called the captains in for a meeting and status update.

"Everybody's here, Jeannie," smiled Amanda.

"Thank you, Mandy, but you've been on leave, where's your second?"

"I'll call her in," grinned Amanda as she reached for her comm. "Commander Morthel to the bridge."

"On my way," came the lilting reply.

She soon arrived, wearing Commander's insignia on her uniform. "As acting captain of EX2 I'd like you to sit in on this meeting Morthel."

"Of course, Admiral." She saluted and sat beside Amanda.

"Now then, people, report, what is the state of your ships?"

"Recovery ships are good to go, Admiral," replied Olga Volkov.

"Friendship is good as new," smiled Linsey.

"Retriever has been fully repaired, the crew is hale and sound, Admiral. We're good to go," said Sheila.

"Reacher and EX4 are ready, Admiral."

"Thank you, Captain Moore. F1 is good to go. Morthel, how is our poor EX2 doing?"

"EX2 is still in the repair bay, Admiral. The repairs are mostly finished, but some of the new augments are taking a bit more time to get properly aligned."

"New augments?"

Rhonda sighed. "I'll answer that one, Morthel. Admiral, Engineering has made some improvements in the designs. They plan to test the new weapons systems with EX2 before trying to install them on the rest of the fleet. They also noted where the structure failed under fire and have reinforced those areas somewhat. Do you want me to call in the chief engineer for a more detailed report?"

"No, that's fine, Rhonda. You and I can visit Moira once were done here. Linsey, how did the negotiations go?"

"We got some new and different foodstuffs; Commander Peters is working on integrating some of that now. We also got full access to the ship's main computers, downloaded a wealth of information, but otherwise didn't disturb their temple ship.

"Admiral, I should tell you, both Ka'Ron and the chief engineer believe we could resurrect that ship. She was a battleship of the Morar, just not able to stand up to the Wrax. What do you want to do here?"

Jeannie sighed and leaned back in her chair. "That ship isn't ours; neither is it salvage. We leave it as is. However, it brings me to my next plan. I know we're going to run into more aggressive species as we go along. If not, then happy days. If we do, I want to be ready."

"Jeannie, what are you thinking?" asked Captain Baris.

"The Reacher isn't a battleship, she's a home, a home for a number of decimated species, an incubator for our collective survival. Our only real protection is the shields, a few improvised weapons, and a few small ships we've salvaged or built.

"I want us to find a sister ship for Reacher, a big sister to fight the battles if necessary. I want something more powerful, something that could, in theory, stand up to a full Wrax ship. There's no more room to carry more ships inside the Reacher, so we'll need something big enough to fly beside her."

"Jeannie, what are you doing now?" sighed her grandfather.

"That's an easy one, Captain Baris," grinned Rhonda. "She's trying to take the pressure off me and better protect the people at the same time. I've got a ship full of bored people, no jobs for them, nothing useful for most of the to do. Bored people get into trouble, cause trouble.

"Now, a sister ship, a battleship, would need crew, lots of jobs openings, plenty of useful things to do, plus it would offer greater protection and as such greatly increase our chances of survival overall. Did I get it right, Admiral?"

"You did, Rhonda. That was the best case scenario. We can't take the one down there, so I thought we could return to the Rift Planet, see what we can find there. As I recall, the chief engineer wanted to stay and see what other wonders were free-floating around that planet."

"Yes but haven't the Wrax destroyed anything useful back there?" asked Olga Volkov.

"There were a lot of ships floating around, back there, perhaps we could find one we could salvage," mused Linsey. "While you folks worked at that, I could add a dozen more languages to my database; make the translator a lot faster."

Jeannie smiled at that. "So, what do you think, people, is it worth a shot?"

"Let's do it," grinned Captain Baris. "It's not like we have anywhere else to be right now, we're topped up for food and fuel. If we need more metals and new tech, there's a wealth of them back there."

"So, we're agreed then?"

"It's your call, Admiral, but I believe we're all in agreement with you," smiled her grandfather.

"Then we go. Captain Moore, prepare your ship for interstellar travel, destination Rift Planet. Don't wait for me, as soon as you're ready, take us back there."

"Aye, Admiral," grinned Rhonda, as she stood to go, "Rift Planet all possible speed."

* * * * *

Once again a young, untried, captain stood on the bridge of the Reacher. "All small ships aboard and locked down, Reacher locked down and ready for travel, Captain. Course is laid in and star drive is online."

"Hit it," she grinned. The mighty Reacher shuddered slightly, then vanished from the skies of the Morar world.

* * * * *

Back on the world of the Morar, Ka'Ron stood in conference with the chieftains and the elder priest. "Do you seriously believe we can do this, Ancient Ka'Ron?" asked the old fellow, as he leaned heavily on his walking stick.

"I do, Honored Elder. It will take much time. First I must teach the chosen how to read the manuals, then we must apply what is learned to making repairs, but with time and diligence, the Morar can return to the stars once again."

* * * * *

Two weeks later, the Reacher reappeared amid the floating derelicts around the Rift Planet. Jeannie called the captains together for a conference. "All right, people, we're here. Amanda, head for the second planet in the Goldilocks Zone, see if you can find us a whole ship to salvage. Sheila, go with her as shotgun.

"Olga, take your two ships out and start exploring some of these derelicts, gather up what tech you can find, bring back anything at all that you think might be useful. Jake, send out EX4 to ride shotgun for them.

"Rhonda, tell your engineering department to get ready, they're going to be busy, and soon."

"They'll be happy to hear it, Admiral." With that she rose, saluted, and headed for Engineering, a smile of delight on her face. She was finally confident that the admiral wouldn't try to interfere in the running of her ship. Captain Rhonda Moore was a happy woman.

The End

Author: And now for a peek at the next book in this series, Fleet.

FLEET

by
Prudence MacLeod

Chapter 1

Salvage

Allissandra Morgenstern sighed as she gazed at her reflection in the mirror of her small quarters. She wasn't old, but not so young anymore either. "Well, now what? You're single again, or should I say still, because it's felt like that for a long while now. So, today you finally got that promotion you've wanted for years, why aren't you happy?

"Oh, just shut up, Alli. Go to sleep and wake up happy, start the new life tomorrow." With another deep sigh, and self-admonition, she dimmed the light, softened the music, then climbed into the small bunk and closed her eyes. Sleep was a long time coming, the tears weren't.

* * * * *

The last starship, Reacher, began to slow down as she neared her destination. Both Admiral Suvi-jean Sorenson and Reacher's new captain, Captain Rhonda Moore, were on the bridge. Jeannie smiled as she listened to the voices of the bridge crew.

"We've dropped to sub-light speed, Captain."

"Shields."

"Shields are up, Captain."

"All stop."

"All stop, aye. Ship has stopped, Captain."

"Sensors, is there any sign of life anywhere in this system?"

"None so far, Captain."

"Anita, can you identify the remains of the Wrax ship?" asked Suvi-jean.

"It's in close orbit to the first planet in the Goldilocks Zone, Admiral. No life signs on it, and no indication it has power."

"I don't trust those bastards," muttered Jeannie, as she reached for her comm unit. "Sorenson to Captain Singh."

"Here, Admiral."

"Ready your crew, you're going back to the Wrax ship to see what's what, I'll bring Fighter One and ride shotgun for you."

"Understood."

"Sorenson to SUVI 9."

"Here, Five."

"Ready F1, we're going out."

"Understood."

"Rhonda, hold your position until you hear from me. I want to make doubly certain that damn ship is dead, and there are no nasty surprises waiting for us."

"Understood, Admiral. I'll ask Anita to poke around with the sensors, see if there's anything else interesting out there while you're gone."

Suvi-jean smiled as she left the bridge, heading for the launch bay. Rhonda turned back to the big forward screen and gazed at the sea of wreckage slowly orbiting that planet. "Commander Jones, warm up the forward cannon and target that Wrax ship, you know, just in case our people need to make a fast exit."

"Aye, Captain," replied the second officer. He motioned with his hand and the gunner flipped the switch to arm the weapon.

A few moments later the man spoke. "Weapon is armed, target acquired, Commander."

"Well done, gunner. Maintain status until further orders."

"Aye, Commander, maintaining status."

"All set, Captain."

"And now we wait," said Rhonda, as she locked her gaze on the forward screen. They watched as the two small ships appeared on screen, streaking toward the derelict ship. The two ships buzzed around it for a few minutes, then one disappeared inside.

* * * * *

The ship, Retriever, settled to the partially buckled deck of the Wrax warship. "Ship has landed, Captain Singh."

"You're up, Hal. Go see if there's anything interesting on this thing."

"Aye, Captain. Kumar, anything moving on sensors?"

"Not a thing, Commander."

"Good to know. Suit up, people. We'll move in two teams; Sessas, you're with me, we'll take point. Billy, Rayla, you're with Twenty, you guys watch our backs." With that, he fastened down his helmet then led them into the airlock.

They were back in the cargo bay of the Wrax ship, but there were plenty of new damage signs, not there when they'd last entered that warship. "Retriever, there's no atmosphere, so unlikely there's anybody left alive over here. Looks like maybe a dozen of their fighter ships left we could salvage. On our way to check out the cryo room now."

"Understood. Be careful, Hal."

"Roger that," came his reply. A short while later he reported in again. "Retriever, cryo room empty, everything powered down, no life signs anywhere. Moving on."

"Understood."

A long while later he checked in again. "Retriever, much of the ship is inaccessible due to damage, the bridge is still intact, but no signs of life and no power anywhere. I'd say she's clear for salvage."

"Understood, Commander White, return to the ship. Retriever calling F1."

"Sorenson here, what's the good word, Sheila?"

"No signs of life, and no atmosphere, Admiral, maybe a dozen small fighters intact and Hal says the bridge survived. They believe she's ready for salvage if you want."

"I do want. Sheila, have your people watch over the salvage crews, just in case. I'll go home and send Olga over."

"Understood, Admiral. Retriever out." Captain Sheila Singh turned to her crew and smiled. "All right, crew, might as well relax, it'll take her a while to get things organized. We'll catch a rest while we can."

* * * * *

On the admiral's personal fighter ship, F1, Suvi-jean was smiling. "Six, take us home."

"Homeward bound, Five."

The Earalith ship, F1, moved swiftly away from the huge wreck and returned to Reacher to make a soft landing in the cargo bay. They barely touched down when Jeannie threw open the hatch and headed for the bridge, already on the comms. "Sorenson to Captain Volkov."

"Olga here, Jeannie."

"Sheila says it's ready to salvage. I'll ask Rhonda to send Moira over with you to have a look."

"Recovery One ready for flight and standing by, Admiral."

"Sorenson to Captain Moore."

"Here, Admiral."

"The wreck is ready to salvage. I'd like Moira to have a look at it, see what we can learn from it that might be useful. I've got Recovery One standing by if you're okay with this."

"I'll send her on her way, Admiral," replied Captain Moore. "Bridge to Engineering."

"Moira here, Rhonda. What's up?"

"Recovery One is standing by if you want to go over and have a look at the Wreck of the Wrax."

"On my way, Captain," came the excited reply.

"Moira, maybe take a few extra hands with you, you know, just in case you find anything useful."

"Understood and appreciated, Captain. Moira out."

"The Wreck of the Wrax?" grinned Jeannie, as she entered the bridge where Rhonda was watching the screen with Emmet and First Officer Brandon Hoffman. "Did I hear that right?"

"Sorry, Admiral, but it was too good to pass up," chuckled Rhonda. "Admiral, while you were gone I had a thought."

"Oh? Care to share?"

"We're here on a salvage mission, correct?"

"Absolutely."

"So, how about I temporarily assign Moira and some of the engineering department to you so they can oversee the main salvage operation, and you don't have to route everything through me. The main areas of Engineering could be designated to them as a salvage area under your direct command as well."

"I like it, Rhonda. Do it, and as soon as we're done here, I'll give them back."

Rhonda chuckled as she turned to Brandon. "First Officer, when the chief engineer returns, confer with her and get this set up for the admiral."

"Aye, Captain. With your permission I'll head down to Engineering and scout out the situation." She nodded, he grinned and winked at Jeannie as he walked off the bridge.

Rhonda smiled then spoke again. "Gunner, I believe we can stand down the weapon now."

"Disengaging weapon, aye. Weapon at rest, Captain."

Jeannie quirked an eyebrow at her. "Rhonda?"

"We had the Wrax ship targeted, just in case. I admit I like a bit of excitement, but I'm a cautious woman nonetheless."

Jeannie smiled brightly at her. "I knew you were the right one for the job. So, is there anything else moving out there?"

Rhonda turned to the woman on sensors. "Anita?"

"Nothing moving under its own power, Captain."

"Then we're set to go," said Jeannie, reaching for her comm. "Sorenson to Captain Drake."

"Amanda here."

"You're clear to go, Mandy. See if you can find me something good."

"Explorer Two is on the hunt," came her reply. Jeannie smiled at the excitement in her lover's voice.

"Admiral, how long do you expect us to be here?" asked Rhonda.

"Months, maybe years, Rhonda. It's hard to say. Come on, let's go to the mess and I'll give you an overview of what I hope to accomplish here."

Rhonda followed her to the mess where they each picked up a mug of the Earalithian tea and a snack. When they'd settled at the table Jeannie picked up the thread of the conversation.

"The Wrax taught us we're vulnerable, we need to up our defenses. This system is a unique gift in that there are literally dozens of ships for us to salvage.

"We can learn so much here, improve our tech, learn new designs, new types of weaponry, defensive shielding, ways to improve engine speed, ship mobility, and so much more. With luck, Amanda will find us a battleship we can repair; if not, then we'll have to build our own.

"We won't leave this system until we've picked it clean of useful information and material."

Rhonda sighed and lowered her mug to the table. "So, we're here for the long haul, now hit me with the bad news. You're going to pillage my crew, aren't you?"

Jeannie chuckled at that. "Somewhat, yes. I want you to work closely with me on this. That ship will need a full crew, and that crew will need ways to return to Reacher to spend time with friends and family."

"Jeannie?"

"Think of Reacher as the home planet. We have small ships for exploration and defense, but we need something more, a big sister to watch over Reacher. Sadly, the crew of that sister ship will not get home like the crews of the small ships do, they'll be living on the new ship.

"For example, she'll need a captain. I can't send Jake; his wives are here and not easily transferred. Carla is your chief of medical and I want her there, so Jake can't be offered the post."

"How about Hal? He'd be good."

"Lilly is attached to EX2."

"So, no Hal?"

"I won't separate families unless there is no other choice," replied Jeannie.

"What about Sheila, her new love interest could go with her."

"I like it. Sheila is a strong possibility, and Hal could captain Retriever. Yes, I like it. Okay, you've got the idea, mull it over for a while, talk to your senior staff about it and I'll do the same with the captains. There's no hurry. It could be a couple of years before we get to that stage."

"But we will get there," mused Rhonda, "so we might as well start grooming people for the new positions. For example, the new ship will need a security department. That team will have to be mined from Jake's crew. He'll need to start training people for those positions. Carla will have to start grooming people for the medical staff."

"I was right, you're going to rob me blind. How many people do you think you'll need?"

Jeannie chuckled. "Let's wait and see what we come up with for a ship." With that she rose and left the mess hall.

Rhonda stood, took the trays to the rack then leaned across the counter to thank the kitchen staff for the meal.

Don't miss out!

Visit the website below and you can sign up to receive emails whenever Prudence MacLeod publishes a new book. There's no charge and no obligation.

https://books2read.com/r/B-A-ZKBBB-JCQQC

BOOKS 2 READ

Connecting independent readers to independent writers.

Also by Prudence MacLeod

Forgotten Worlds
Suvi
Echo of the Past
Survivors
Ship

Watch for more at https://www.prudencemacleod.com/.

About the Author

Jennifer Crandall writes and publishes under three different names, Prudence MacLeod, J.L.Crandall, and Jenni Leigh. Learn more about her on her website,

Read more at https://www.prudencemacleod.com/.

www.ingramcontent.com/pod-product-compliance
Lightning Source LLC
Chambersburg PA
CBHW020947180626
46814CB00003B/971